GREYSANDS

MARK EDMONDSON

Greysands

Published by The Conrad Press in the United Kingdom 2020

Tel: +44(0)1227 472 874
www.theconradpress.com
info@theconradpress.com

ISBN 978-1-911546-98-6

Typesetting and Cover Design by: Charlotte Mouncey, www.bookstyle.co.uk

Cover image created with designers own images and details from photos of sand dunes by herprettybravesoul.com and sky by Emma Francis both available on www.unsplash.com, and photo of amusement park by Christian Horz on www.istockphoto.com

The Conrad Press logo was designed by Maria Priestley.

For Maggi

'This is the coastal town,
that they forgot to close down.'

Morrissey

1

'Would you like to look around on your own, Mr Lloyd?' the young lady asked.

Philip gazed through the large bay window. The view was amazing. He could see for miles over the ocean. The tide was high and making its way to the dry sand and scattered pebbles. To the right, if he leaned closer to the window, he could see the large grassy hill where the red-bricked lighthouse stood. The dark grey clouds held onto the rain for now, but it didn't look as though it would be long before the heavens opened. The gloomy scene of a ghostly and dying seaside town was the perfect place for Philip Lloyd to be. He'd already made his decision.

Greysands was a small seaside town in Lancashire nestled between Blackpool and Lancaster. There was only one road in and one road out of the forgotten town that was littered with closed signs and boarded-up shop-fronts. Some businesses were still hanging on. The pub and the cafe were still open. The lights of the arcade at the edge of the promenade were still flashing. The chip shop was still trading and the grocery store was still open. But the novelty gift shops were all but gone. The miniature railway tracks were rusted and the ornamental fountains were green with algae.

The beautiful, natural scenery of the town wasn't going to be enough to keep the businesses going. It was considered by many a good place to get some peace and quiet, or to walk the dog along the beach. But the single road that brought people here was eight miles from any other passing routes. The town wasn't on the way anywhere, and it wasn't going to compete with the bright lights of Blackpool or the sandy beaches of Lytham St Annes. The arcade lights were like dying embers compared to the illuminations further down the coastline. Although Philip Lloyd found this a little sad, he also found it fascinating. He wondered what characters lived in a small town like this, and what secrets they might be hiding. Who was still here and who had got away? He imagined Greysands was the kind of town where nobody wanted to live, as beautiful as it was. He thought that as soon as the kids were old enough, most of them probably took flight.

It was the perfect place to write his next novel. And he wasn't going to get a more perfect house to rent than this one, especially one that was fully furnished. As he stared through the window, he knew this was the place for him. It was the perfect place to write, and it was the perfect place to escape the past. He knew the past always had a habit of catching up with you, and he knew there was still unfinished business back at home, but out here in this ghostly town, he thought he might just have a chance of breaking free and starting again. He wasn't sure if that was what he wanted, but it certainly felt like the right thing to do; for now, at least.

'Mr Lloyd.'

'Hmm.'

'Would you like to look around on your own?'

He brought his mind back to the job in hand. 'No. I don't need to look around. I'll take it.'

The young lady looked surprised.

She had told him her name but he couldn't remember it. She didn't look old enough to work as an estate agent. He thought she was about twenty, she could've been older, but not by much.

'Don't you want to see the other rooms?'

The living room had a very old-fashioned feel to it. The carpet had a brown and gold pattern that looked as though it was laid four decades earlier. But there was a real log fire, with a wood pile stacked in the alcove, a comfortable looking sofa and a large desk in front of the bay window.

'No. It's perfect.'

'Do you want to see the bedrooms at least?'

At first Philip's overactive imagination thought she might be suggesting something, but when he turned to look at her, he saw an innocent expression of youth on her young smiling face. Her long dark hair gave her a Mediterranean look, but her accent was one hundred percent Lancashire. As he turned to judge her gaze, he caught a glimpse of himself in the large mirror that was hanging on the wall in the alcove next to the stone fireplace. When he saw his grey hair, pale complexion and tired eyes, he quickly realised that the young woman was being anything but suggestive.

His confidence in talking to the ladies had been met with some surprising results over the years; when he was a police officer, he'd been propositioned many times, and quite a few times after becoming a successful author, although he wasn't as flattered by then as the women who showed an interest in him knew of his success. But now at fifty-five years old, he thought that maybe he should stop thinking of himself as a ladies' man, especially considering the situation he'd recently fallen into.

'No. This is just right.'

'Mr Lloyd, the views at the back aren't quite in the same league as the views from this window.'

'I'm sure they're not. Nothing beats a sea view, even on a cold winter's day like this.'

'Mr Lloyd,' she suddenly became more serious and her smile dispersed from her face. 'Please come upstairs? You'll see what I mean.'

They walked through the living room door and climbed the wooden stairs that creaked with every step. The hallway at the top of the stairs was very dark and smelled of damp. This didn't bother him too much because he wasn't looking to buy the property, he was only looking to rent. Any building repairs wouldn't be his problem, and he also guessed that the property might've been empty for some time.

Once upstairs, he followed the young woman to the end of the hall. She opened the door and they walked into a very dark and depressing room. There was a single bed, a wooden chair and a dark wooden wardrobe. The light-blue curtains were drawn, but the daylight came through them and dimly lit the room.

She stood in front of the curtains and turned back to face him. 'This is the part you might not like.'

'OK,' he said. He knew he had an overactive imagination; he got paid a lot of money for it; but he had no clue what she was about to reveal to him.

She reached up and slid the curtains open. Suddenly, her reservations made sense to him. He stepped forward to look through the window. He saw a decent sized garden of about fifteen feet in length. There was an overgrown grass lawn that was surrounded by a concrete fence, but that wasn't what she was showing him. On the other side of the fence was probably to most people the most depressing scene anyone could imagine. But Philip felt a breathlessness at what he could see. Now he knew for sure that this was the house for him.

He looked down on an area the size of two football fields, surrounded by large iron fencing. It was an amusement park. He could tell it'd been closed for many years by the way all the grassed areas were overgrown and the rides and machinery were full of cancerous rust.

A large metal wheel that once spun swings around had years of rust building up on the framework and the swings lay dormant, hanging just above the forest of weeds. The merry-go-round was full of bird droppings and the painted flowers on the carts were all faded to a pale white. The rollercoaster track was rusted and overgrown with weeds and the entrance to the ride was a blue hut that was now partially covered with flaking paint. The pond in the middle was home to a family of large plastic swan-shaped pedalos that were dirty with algae. One of them floated on its side, partially under the surface of the water. And the Waltzer was barely visible under the bushes and weeds that had consumed most of the park.

Philip could see why she wanted him to see the full picture. She didn't know that to Philip, this would be the best thing about the house. The old and dingy house that his wife Lesley certainly wouldn't have agreed to even stay in for a week's holiday, let alone a year, was perfect for him, even though he was aware that most people would consider it to be an eyesore. He was now starting to realise why the estate agent sent her.

'What's your name again?' he asked.

'Jenny,' she said.

'And how old are you?'

'Twenty-two.'

'How many people work in your office?'

'Eight of us,' she said, looking confused at his line of questioning.

'And this is a question that I've managed to avoid asking for the full twenty-five years of my career, but I'm afraid I'm going to have to ask it now.'

'OK,' she said, still looking perplexed.

'Do you know who I am?'

She smiled a little. 'No.'

'But the people above you told you that I was a big deal, didn't they?'

She nodded in a coy way, looking down at the ground as she did.

'You were told to show me around and be as nice as you can to me and thankfully, you were told to make me aware of everything, but to keep smiling that beautiful smile of yours.'

She blushed a little, but nodded again.

He smiled at her. 'I'm sure this house has been viewed by many people who loved the front but hated the back.'

'It has.'

'Well you can ring your office and tell them you've clinched the deal.'

Her eyebrows lifted. 'Really?'

'Yes. Give them a ring and tell them that the ugly old mongrel that nobody wanted has just found a new master. At the rental price it's up at.'

Her smile widened as she took her phone out of her pocket

and walked out of the room. It was at that point that Philip realised her previous smiles were fake. She now smiled a real smile as her face lit up as soon as the sentence left his lips. Jenny was going to get her commission and Philip was going to get a twelve-month stay in a house that was ugly and old-fashioned, but in the perfect location. This house and this town were the perfect place to inspire his next story, and the perfect place for a new beginning. For the first time in a long time, he felt excited.

2

The following Monday, the thirteenth of January, Philip pulled his black Mercedes up outside of the house that was just as he remembered it. Only today it looked even more impressive to him as the roof and gardens were covered in at least four inches of snow. The roads had been cleared a little by previous traffic, but the pavements were untouched. Even though it was only just after nine, he was still surprised to see nobody around as he'd driven through the town. He wondered if the locals used a snow storm as an excuse to stay at home. Or maybe the shops and the cafe didn't open until later anyway. These were all things he was going to have to find out so he could settle into the town and learn the ways of the locals.

He stood next to his car and looked up at the house before saying to himself, 'Well, Philip, set your watch back thirty years; you're home.'

This house was very different to the one he'd bought after his writing career took off and he became a success. This house didn't have a swimming pool, or a kitchen island, and it definitely didn't have a state-of-the-art security system or even Wi-Fi. But in a strange, nostalgic way, going back in time made him feel happy. He loved the fact that he was a successful author, but the thrill of being able to buy anything he wanted had worn off within the first year or so since his first best-selling novel brought him his fortune. He was glad to get back to reality.

He'd brought his clothes in cardboard boxes and a toiletry bag with his razors, shaving foam, shower gel and deodorant inside. He hadn't brought any food or even tea bags or milk. He decided that he'd get supplies from the local grocery store, thinking this would be a good way to meet his first local.

As he put his last cardboard box down on the floor at the bottom of the stairs, a voice made him jump.

'Good morning.'

He spun around to see a man standing on his doorstep. He was dressed in a thick winter coat, wellington boots and had a dog with him. The dog looked like a greyhound, only it was a lot smaller.

'Are you the new tenant, sir?' he asked.

The man was stocky, barrel-chested and bald, but had a friendly look on his face. Philip also noticed he was holding his bobble hat, which he thought was a gentlemanly thing to do. He always remembered his father removing his hat whenever he spoke to anybody.

'I am,' Philip said. He then offered his hand out. 'Philip ...' he almost said his last name but thought better of it. He thought he'd try to keep a low profile for now, and not let anyone know he was a reasonably famous, but very successful author. 'Philip's the name.'

The man shook his hand. 'Nice to meet you. I'm Tom Dawson. I'm probably the only person you'll ever see walk by your house.'

'Really? Why's that?'

'I'm the lighthouse keeper. I work from three until nine in the winter; longer hours in the summer.'

'I didn't realise lighthouses were still used.'

'They are still used, but this one stopped being used back in two thousand and two. Because of the shape of the coastline almost being like an estuary, ships don't come close to our shore so it's thought of by the *powers at be* that it's not needed anymore. And although fishing is still a big part of the town's income, the harbour is two miles down the coastline, so this lighthouse is about as much use as a sixty-year-old fellow with a whippet. But I have a deal with the council. If I can raise the funds to keep it going and do the maintenance myself, they'll keep providing the power for a limited number of hours a day.'

'Really?'

'Yes. For the tourists, you know? Not that we get many.'

Philip found that fascinating. The lighthouse was a beautiful building. It would be a shame for it to go unused.

'Where have you emigrated from, if you don't mind me asking?'

'Emigrated?' Philip asked. 'I haven't emigrated. I'm from Chorley, not far from Manchester.'

'Oh, you have,' Tom said. 'Pretty soon you'll feel as though you've moved to another country, especially coming from a busy place like Manchester.'

His house in Chorley was actually twenty-five miles from Manchester. But he was used to telling people during his book tours where he was from and not many people knew where Chorley was. He found it easier to just say Manchester.

'I was hoping to get away from the rat race. I thought this was the perfect house in the perfect town.'

Tom Dawson raised his eyebrows. 'I don't know about perfect, but it'll certainly feel like you're away from the rat race.'

'Hopefully,' Philip said. 'I'd offer you a drink but I haven't anything in as yet.'

'No, that's fine. I was just saying hello on my way past. Karen's will be open at eleven. That's Greysands Groceries. She lives above, so she won't have trouble getting through the snow like some of the other businesses.'

'Thanks. I'll go and get stocked up as soon as she opens.'

'Well,' Tom said, 'welcome to the town, and I hope you settle in.'

'I'll do my best.'

They shook hands once more before Tom turned away. 'Nice to meet you,' he said. He then said over his shoulder, 'Lock your doors,' as he began to walk down the path.

This surprised Philip. It was said in a jovial manner, almost like a 'see you later.' He couldn't let this go unquestioned.

'Lock my doors?' he asked.

Tom stopped and turned back. 'Yes.' He then seemed to struggle to find what to say. 'Yes. It's just an expression; a saying we have.'

Philip was even more confused.

'Bye for now,' Tom said. 'Come on, Daisy.'

All Philip could think as he watched the old man walk away through the snow, was what a strange thing to say to somebody you'd just met, and what a stupid name for a whippet.

3

After unpacking his clothes, Philip put on his coat and flat cap – hoping this would act as a disguise – and locked the front door, as Tom had said to, before setting off through the snow on foot to get some supplies.

It was eleven o'clock by now so he thought the grocery store should be open. He hadn't had a cup of tea since seven o'clock that morning, so he was ready to knock on the door if necessary. Tea was his addiction. Ever since he became a writer, he always had to have a cup of tea on his desk, even though they'd sometimes go cold while he was experiencing an overload of inspiration. He also found making the cup of tea a therapeutic break from the flicker of the computer screen as he gathered his thoughts. Tea bags would definitely be his first purchase.

The sun was up by now, although it was still bitterly cold. He looked to his right to take in the view of the impressive building that was the lighthouse. He looked forward to nightfall so he could see it in action. He also wondered if Tom would let him climb the steps one day and see inside. He'd never been inside a lighthouse before and thought it would be an interesting experience.

He turned left at the bottom of the path and made his way along the pavement towards the town. There was no wind so the sea was quiet and the tide was a good four hundred yards from the beach. He was impressed by the stunning scenery and couldn't help but think he'd made a good choice in Greysands.

He hoped he would continue to feel this way.

He walked past the pub first. It was only a small pub; the end of a row of terraced buildings. The cafe was next door. Then he came to the grocery store. His face was starting to hurt with the cold. He was relieved to see the lights on and the LED *Open* sign flashing away.

Philip went into the shop and once again, he felt as though he'd gone back in time. The shop floor had grey speckled tiles, and the shelving was wooden, handmade and solidly built, but must've been erected decades ago. Every item had an individual orange price-gun label, and some of the shelves had handwritten special offers on luminous star-shaped cards. The bread was next to the canned foods, but then there was a shelf full of cheap children's toys, and the other was filled with cereal boxes. As he walked around the corner, he saw a scatter of eclectic products ranging from padlocks to shoe polish. There were car sponges, air fresheners, Allen keys, and then a small selection of stationery. The yellow fluorescent lights revealed a shop that seemed to sell everything, but with owners who had no idea of product display or retail management. If there was a space for it, then that was where it went.

'Welcome to Greysands,' he heard a friendly voice say.

He turned around to see a woman, possibly in her fifties. She had short brown hair, in an unkempt style, and a face that was pretty, but could've been prettier if she'd bothered to apply just a little makeup.

'Oh. Good morning.'

'How are you settling in at the park house?' she asked as she walked behind the counter and closed the flap.

Philip was confused once more. 'How did you ...' he began.

'It's January. Nobody comes here in January. Don't you think I know everyone in this town?'

Philip laughed. 'I suppose a grocery store is the perfect place to keep abreast of what's going on.'

'It is that.'

Philip noticed a book shelf next to the counter. The first book he noticed was one of his, *Time for Departure*. It was his third release, so he was surprised to see such an old book for sale. When he looked again, he realised that they were all second-hand, and only a pound each. This saddened him a little, although he would've certainly already had his royalties from the original sale of the copy, so it didn't bother him too much.

He didn't mention it to the woman. He wanted to keep his career to himself for now. He didn't necessarily mind people knowing he was a writer, but he didn't want them to know how successful. He also wanted to keep things to himself, should his recent indiscretion become public. He hoped that it hadn't made the news yet, and if it did, that maybe the Internet didn't exist in this part of the world. He knew that wouldn't be the case, but looking around this shop, he thought it was a possibility.

'I'm Philip,' he said, approaching her to shake her hand.

'Nice to meet you, Philip. I'm Karen. Welcome to the back of beyond.'

'Thank you very much.' He started to grab items from the shelves and place them on the counter. 'How long have you lived in Greysands?'

She laughed as she typed the items into the till before bagging them. 'I wouldn't waste any time asking anyone that question if I were you.'

'Why's that?'

'Everyone who lives in Greysands was born in Greysands. People don't move here; they move away from here.'

'Well I've just moved here,' he said.

'Yeah, give it time.'

'Don't newcomers last?'

'Never.'

He stopped looking for items and stepped back towards the counter. 'Is it not a very welcoming town?'

'Oh, the locals are very welcoming; most of them anyway. It's just that this town isn't a very exciting town to live in. Most of the kids move on elsewhere the first chance they get. I don't know of anyone who's moved here and stayed here. But there's always a first.'

'I'll consider that a challenge,' he said, smiling.

He did another circuit of the shop, collecting more items before taking them to the counter. The last thing he chose was a chocolate fudge cake in a blue cardboard box. He always abstained from alcohol while working on a novel, so when he was dry, he liked to replace the drink with something else a little naughty, and there was nobody to tell him off for it now. He knew this cake wouldn't last very long.

She packed everything up for him. 'Thirty-two fifty-three, if you please?'

He handed the money over and took a hold of the four full carrier bags. 'Well, nice to meet you,' he said. 'And thanks for the friendly welcome.'

'No problem at all, Philip. I hope you settle in and enjoy your stay.'

'I'll do my best.' He walked to the door.

Karen trotted around and opened it for him.

'Thanks. See you later.'

'Yes. Bye now. Lock your doors,' she said, just as she closed the door.

This sentence caused him to stop in his tracks again, but as he turned around, he saw through the glass door that Karen had already walked away.

'Lock your doors,' he muttered to himself as he walked back towards his house.

4

The carrier bags dug into his fingers as he opened the front door of his new house, so he put them onto the floor as soon as he could. As he closed the door, he heard another one slam shut somewhere in the house. His heart raced as he quickly tried to decide where the noise came from. It could've been the back door, but it also could've come from upstairs. He wasn't sure.

He stepped over the bags and ran alongside the staircase and into the kitchen. He tried the handle on the back door. It was locked. He looked at the windows that were firmly shut, but also holding a few inches of snow on the bottom of the frames. If the windows had been slammed, surely the snow would have fallen.

He turned and ran back towards the front door, then spun himself around by grabbing onto the banister and running up the stairs as fast as his fifty-five-year-old legs would take him.

He checked the master bedroom at the front of the house. Nothing. He checked the second bedroom and the bathroom. Still nothing. Whatever he'd heard could only have come from the third bedroom, the one at the rear of the property that looked out over the amusement park.

He slowly approached the closed door, listening for any more noises. There was nothing he could hear other than the creaking of the old floorboards that moved with every step. He reached for the handle. He turned it slowly and took a deep breath before pushing the door open and rushing into the room.

Nothing.

The room was as empty as it was the last time he saw it, when the young estate agent showed it to him. He walked over to the window and pulled the curtains back to check the window. It was closed.

He looked out over the amusement park. The untouched snow looked beautiful as it shielded the rusted and neglected rides from view. The pond was frozen over, and the park looked deserted of all life.

He turned around and made his way back down the stairs. Once at the bottom, he stood over the carrier bags once more before opening the front door. He then slammed it shut, listening for any other bangs.

Nothing.

He wondered if the backdraft of the door closing caused one of the internal doors in the house to slam shut; either way, his house was empty and his doors were locked.

Still panting, he took the shopping through to the kitchen so he could make himself some breakfast, and a much-needed cup of tea.

5

After he'd eaten and cleaned the kitchen, Philip decided it was time to set up his computer and think about starting work on his next DI Lauren Bates novel. He'd brought his laptop with him. He didn't see the point of bringing his PC. The tower and large monitor were hard to move and set up, and took up valuable space in his car. The laptop was all he needed for now.

He plugged in the lead and fired it up. As he sat there at the desk in front of the large bay window, he looked out to sea at the stunning scenery and thought how lucky he was to find this house. He'd already lit the fire, and made a fresh cup of tea, so he now felt ready. He took a deep breath; it was now time to focus on rebuilding his career.

His agent, Daniel, had bugged him for years to get a mobile phone but Philip refused. He didn't see the point of them and liked the fact that he was probably the only person he knew that didn't own one. Even his mum and dad had one each when they were alive. The fact that they aren't just phones anymore was supposed to be a good thing, but why on earth would he need a camera, a torch or a computer in his pocket the whole time? He liked the fact that he could go out in the afternoon or evening and not get interrupted by anyone. There were always a handful of messages on his answer phone when he returned, but he could deal with them when he was ready, and on his own terms.

Philip knew he'd have to sort a landline out for this new house, but for now, it was a relief for him to be out of reach of everyone from his old life. Daniel had his address, but he lived an hour away in Manchester. His wife Lesley, had told him not to contact her. She'd said she would phone him once she was ready to talk, but he didn't think that this would mean they'd be getting back together. She was a proud woman and he knew she'd never forgive him. His marriage was all but over, although he hadn't quite given up just yet.

He was also glad that Daniel couldn't get hold of him. He wouldn't be doing any interviews or press for his recently released novel. He wanted everything to settle down first before he showed his face in public again. He decided that he had a year to work on his next book. Everything always felt rushed to him. He was happy he could spend as much time as he wanted getting it up to scratch before sending it to Daniel. He was a little worried about not having any help from Lesley as she always proofread everything for him, and also gave him her ruthless opinion on the manuscript. She always said, *If I don't tell you, your agent will.* And more often than not, she was right.

He'd met Lesley when he was in the police force. She was a social worker who he'd crossed paths with on a few occasions. He already had her card with her phone number in his wallet months before he'd quit the force. He gave her a call a few weeks later and asked if she'd like to go for a meal. She accepted the invitation and they very quickly fell in love. He loved her confidence and her ability to say whatever she wanted; no matter how abrupt it would come across. She wouldn't think twice about sending a meal back in a restaurant, or telling a rude shop assistant to learn some manners. Whereas most people bite their tongue and rant about things after the event, she would always react quickly and deal with the situation there and then. This made him feel more confident about their relationship. He knew that if she was unhappy with him, or even fell out of love with him, she'd make it perfectly clear how she felt.

Philip had wanted to become a police officer ever since he was a child. Watching shows like *Hill Street Blues* and *Starsky and Hutch*, and of course *The Sweeney*, fed his imagination. But the reality of being a police officer wasn't as exciting as it was in the world of fiction. He enjoyed the adrenaline rush whenever he had to deal with a situation, but it never quite fulfilled his ambitions. He had never stopped being a big fan of books, reading more than two a week, so he decided to start writing his own novels.

He was always very good at English, and didn't have to try too hard to learn the techniques. He found an agent quite easily, but his first three novels were rejected by publishers. He refused to give up, and found writing was not only an addictive and therapeutic way to spend his spare time, but also a craft he was getting better and better at.

His fourth attempt was accepted by the first publisher his agent sent it to. It sold a reasonable amount of copies, but only just enough to pay the bills. But his second release became a bestseller, and suddenly Philip Lloyd was a famous name throughout the literary world.

His writing career had taken off at about the same time he and Lesley found out they couldn't have children. Lesley was distraught at the thought of never having any offspring, but Philip just took it in his stride. They talked about adopting, but neither of them felt passionate enough about going down that road to pursue it. Lesley wanted to carry her own child and the fact that she couldn't seemed to put her off having children by any other means. So, it was just the two of them.

They were very happily married. They both enjoyed the wealth his career brought them. Lesley gave up work after his book became a bestseller and from then on took on the role as his personal assistant. She not only read every draft of every novel, but also arranged the book tours, public appearances and interviews. But she wouldn't be helping him from now on. She wasn't going to forgive him for what he'd done. He couldn't see her being involved in his life, let alone his career.

Philip had always fancied himself as a ladies' man. He enjoyed flirting, especially with younger ladies. He found it easier to make a twenty-year-old woman blush than a thirty-year-old who'd heard it all before. On several occasions over the years he'd been propositioned by young female fans. He always answered in the same way; 'I'm very flattered, but I'm a happily married man.' Or, 'I didn't mean to give you the wrong idea, I was just enjoying talking to you.'

This was how he enjoyed his life for twenty-five years. A beautiful wife, a great career and a small group of young ladies that made him feel as though he was something special. He knew he was no Brad Pitt, and he was pretty sure these women wouldn't have found him as attractive if he hadn't had been so successful, but he still enjoyed the attention; even though he had no intention of ever acting upon it.

When Jade Romily came into his life, suddenly everything changed. He met her at a book signing and he was mesmerised by her long dark hair, olive skin, amazing figure and the bluest eyes he'd ever seen. She gazed into his eyes as he sat at the desk and for the first time ever, he was lost for words. She stared at him as he stuttered his way through the signing. She was gorgeous. He still had no intentions of ruining what he had with his wife, but he couldn't take his eyes off her.

That night she'd found him in the hotel bar. She brought over a bottle of champagne and two glasses as he sat there drinking a pint of bitter while reading a book. Philip liked her confidence. He was also blindsided by the fact that she'd brought the bottle over. When he'd been approached before, the women expected him to buy the drinks. Her actions made him feel as though she wasn't after his money and might have actually liked him. He was wrong.

As the evening went on, Philip had worried that he was going to give in to her advances. She kept touching his hands as they talked and rubbed his leg with her feet underneath the table.

It was a relief to him when she said goodnight and left the bar. He was left thinking that it was a lucky escape as he could feel himself drawn to this goddess of a woman.

Half an hour later he made his way to his room, only to find he'd lost his key card. After going down to reception and getting another one, when he opened the door, he was shocked to see Jade Romily standing in his room wearing nothing but a smile, spinning his original card key in her fingers. Her beauty was too much for him to walk away from. He was dizzy with alcohol, but aware enough to know that he was about to do wrong. He just couldn't say no. She was gorgeous. Her body was amazing; her face was as stunning as any supermodel. He was in her trap and he couldn't get out. At that moment his life changed forever.

The guilt weighed heavily on his shoulders for the next two weeks as he continued with the book tour. He always took his laptop on the tours so he could spend the evenings writing, when he wasn't drinking that was. But he couldn't focus on writing; he was torn between coming clean to Lesley or keeping the secret forever. He didn't want to hurt her and he didn't want to lose her. He returned home in late December, and other than feeling incredible guilt, things were fine with him and Lesley all through the Christmas period. But on the Thursday morning of the second of January, four weeks after the event, everything changed.

Philip checked his emails, as he did every morning. He sorted through the junk emails and binned them all before he noticed a name he recognised. Jade Romily. He clicked on the email and saw an attachment for a video. His palms became damp and his heart raced. After a moment of hesitation, he clicked on the video.

He suddenly felt sick as he saw the hotel room. Jade stood naked, and seconds later the door opened and he saw himself walk into the room. The footage was being taken from a stationary camera he presumed was on top of the wardrobe. His hands shook and sweat rolled down his forehead as he watched the full video before exiting the email.

He sat there in disbelief. He thought he was having a nightmare. He then started to doubt what he'd just seen; he wanted to see it again to make sure he wasn't dreaming. After watching it a second time, he exited the video again. His stomach churned. He felt scared. What had happened? More importantly, what was about to happen?

Moments later, another email came through. It was also from

Jade Romily; although he now presumed that wasn't her real name. He opened it. It read, *The entrance of Manchester Town Hall, now. Come alone.*

It was a cold January morning, but the sun was up and it would've been a perfect day in what used to be a perfect life. The drive to Manchester city centre took him over an hour from his house in Chorley. Sitting in traffic jams was something he detested anyway, but wondering what awaited him in Manchester made him more frustrated than ever. He beeped and shouted at other drivers even though they hadn't done much wrong. He just wanted to get it over with; whatever *it* was.

He parked as close as he could to the town hall, about two-hundred yards from the entrance. He walked there at a brisk pace and then waited.

Moments later, Jade Romily walked around the corner. As soon as he saw the smug look on her face, the red mist ascended.

He walked towards her with no idea of what he was going to do when he got there, but his blood was boiling.

Her expression didn't change as he got closer. She put her hands up and calmly said, 'It's broad daylight and my partner has his finger on the button.'

Philip stopped. He knew what she meant about it being broad daylight, but he had no clue what the other comment meant.

'Who are you?' he said, through gritted teeth.

'First of all,' she said, 'look around.'

He stood back and looked at the many people all rushing around the square, all on their way to and from work, he presumed.

'Thanks to modern technology, almost every single person

walking by has a camera in their pocket, and some of them know who you are.'

He didn't speak. His chest rose and fell as his anger built.

'If you don't change your demeanour, someone will film you having an argument with an unknown woman, much younger than you, and share it with the world.'

He knew she was right.

'Now let's sit down and relax as if we're old friends. We kind of are anyway, don't you think?'

She walked a few feet to a park bench in the middle of the square and sat down.

Philip didn't move.

'His finger is on the button. So, I'd sit down if I was you.'

Philip wiped the sweat from his forehead and walked over to the bench, checking all around to see if anyone had spotted him, but nobody had. It was just a normal busy morning to everyone else.

He sat down next to her.

'Right,' she said. 'Let's keep this calm.'

She was dressed like a businesswoman, he thought, in her dark-blue trouser-suit and long crimson raincoat. When he last saw her, she was wearing a short leather skirt and a revealing white blouse, unbuttoned to her cleavage. Today though, she was dressed very professionally.

'That video I sent you is an attached file on an email addressed to your wife. My partner has his finger on the mouse ready to press send if you either assault me or look as though you aren't taking me seriously. Do you understand?'

Philip's jaw was hurting; he was so angry. Never before had he wanted to hit a woman, but he did now. He felt sick. He looked around to see where this second person could be, but he had no clue.

'What do you want from me?' he said.

'I think you can guess,' she said.

He looked at the face he once thought was beautiful and even risked losing his marriage for, but now all he could see was an ugly human being that he wanted to kill. He hoped and prayed for something to happen to make it all stop; a freak burst of lightning, a huge sinkhole appearing, or even a random attack by a stranger; as long as whatever it was, took Jade Romily and not him.

'Money,' he said. More of a statement than a question.

'Got it in one,' she said. She took a packet of cigarettes from her handbag, took one out and lit it.

'I'm not nearly as rich as you think I am,' he said.

She laughed as she blew smoke away from him. 'Is that right?'

'Yes.'

She turned and looked him in the eye. 'So, your last book, *The Playground*, didn't sell two hundred and fifty thousand copies in its first week and then quickly reach three-quarters of million copies within the first month? And your total income last year wasn't about two point five million?'

This made him feel sick. How did she know this?

'You have nine million, three hundred and sixty-four thousand, two hundred and nine pounds and twenty-seven pence in your account as we speak.'

He hadn't checked his account that day, but he knew she was right.

'How do you know all this?'

'It doesn't matter.' She offered him a piece of paper. 'This has a name, account number and sort code written on it. This isn't my account or anyone's who's involved. You go home now and transfer a million pounds to that account and we'll do the rest.'

'The police will know ...'

'It's an account we've hacked. We'll take it straight out and you'll never know where it's gone. If you don't do this within the hour, then we press send.'

'The bank won't let me just transfer ...'

'Yes, they will. You just have to be convincing.'

She got up and walked away.

He watched her leave as he considered his options. He could follow her, but even if she did lead him to her partner, it wouldn't change anything. It was checkmate.

An hour later he returned home. His head was pounding and he was sweating like it was a hot summer's day. He didn't know what to do. He didn't know what choices he had. If he could transfer the money, he would have to tell his accountant where the money had gone. He knew he couldn't just transfer a million pounds and not tell the HMRC.

If he came clean to Lesley, even if he could convince her it was a one-time drunken mistake, she would never forgive him, especially if she actually saw the video. Something like that would stay in her head forever. He also wondered how far this person would go. Would she upload it to the Internet? Once it was on the World Wide Web, it would be there forever. It would ruin his life and his legacy.

If he did pay her, he didn't think that it would be the only payment. She would most certainly ask for more. It could finish him. Was he just prolonging the agony by paying her? What other option was there?

He went onto his computer, the one in his office. He logged onto his online banking and went to the payments page. He typed in the details and the seven-digit amount.

After filling in the details, it looked as though it was about to go through but on the last page of security, a phone number appeared with a message that said transactions of this size need extra security procedures. He phoned the number.

A young man answered and after checking the details and going through all the security questions, he finally asked who the money was for.

Philip told the man that it was a private business arrangement and the man accepted it, and asked if he was happy to proceed.

Philip didn't answer.

He suddenly realised that he was hoping that it wouldn't go through, that he'd have to go into the bank to complete a transaction of this size. But he didn't. He could send her the money and bring the whole situation to an end. A million pounds was a hell of a lot of money, but it wouldn't finish him. All he had to say was go ahead and it would all be over. But would it? Why would she stop? If it's that easy to get so much money from him, why would she stop?

She could take me for all I've got, he thought.

He paused for a moment. There were two options. Pay the money and hope for the best. Or don't pay and hope that Lesley would forgive him and maybe he could beg her to not watch the video. Yes, Jade Romily – definitely not her real name – could upload it to the Internet, but as embarrassing as it would be, it was something that celebrities did all the time. In a strange way it saddened him that this was the world we now live in, and it could actually be helpful to his career.

What he didn't want was to hurt Lesley, but either way, sooner or later she would find out.

He'd made his mind up.

He told the man to cancel it for now and he'd get back to him. He had no intention of getting back to him, though.

He had some apologising to do.

Lesley came home from her morning trip to the gym an hour later. Philip told her what he'd done. She ran upstairs to be sick. Afterwards, she wouldn't speak to him and packed a bag. He stopped her leaving and told her to stay in the house. He said he would go to a hotel, and that they would talk the following day; that he'd do whatever she wanted, but begged her not to check her emails, and to forgive him. She slammed the door in his face.

The next day, Lesley told him to pack as much as he needed and move out as quickly as possible. He spent a week at the hotel, hoping she would change her mind, but she didn't.

He started to realise that he wasn't going to win her over easily.

Lesley said that she couldn't bring herself to look at him and the only chance they had was him moving away and leaving her alone. She told him to find somewhere away from her and everyone they knew and stay away for as long as she felt necessary.

He didn't want to do this but he didn't see any other option. If he wanted her back, he had to do as she wished. He hoped that in his absence she would miss him and want him back. Staying away was his only chance.

6

Philip spent most of the afternoon writing, which surprised him considering it was the first day in his new home. He thought that he'd take a couple of days to get used to his new surroundings before he was firing on all cylinders, but this wasn't the case. He liked to write at least fifteen pages a day when working on a novel that he'd previously planned out. Today, his first full day in Greysands, and he'd managed twenty-two. That was a good start. He was worried that the events of the past week would affect his concentration, but it seemed that it was quite the opposite. He was finding that delving into his make-believe world was a therapeutic escape from the real one.

After sleeping for an hour or so on the old-fashioned sofa, he woke up and stretched before walking over to the window. It was late afternoon by now; the snow was still crisp outside, and the light was beginning to fade.

As he turned the lamp on at side of the desk in front of the window, he saw Tom Dawson walking by with his whippet. He was wrapped up in his winter coat and woollen hat like before. He looked over to the house before waving enthusiastically.

Philip waved back.

At least he knew one friendly face, he thought.

He went into the kitchen and yawned as he filled the kettle for his next cup of tea. As he prepared the cup with the tea bag and his two spoons of sugar, he remembered the chocolate fudge cake. He grabbed a plate from the cupboard and placed it next to the cup and went to get the cake.

He stopped.

He thought he'd left it at the other end of the worktop, but it wasn't there. He checked the cupboards above his head, but couldn't find it. After double-checking all the cupboards and the fridge, he still couldn't find it.

He craved the cake even more now he couldn't find it. He must've left it in the shop. Was it worth getting wrapped up and walking through the snow all the way back to the shop, just to get a sugar fix? He knew the answer to that. He finished his cup of tea and put his coat and hat on.

He walked into the shop, only this time it wasn't empty. There was a man dressed in a blue suit and a long overcoat. He had short, neatly cut, grey hair, set in a side parting. He must've been sixty, but a very healthy sixty. He stood with his hands held in front of him as he spoke to Karen, though he seemed to stop talking as soon as Philip walked into the shop.

Philip felt as though he'd interrupted an argument; Karen looked a little red in the face. She shook it off quickly and forced a smile. 'Hello again, Philip.'

'Good afternoon. Sorry am I interrupting some ...'

The suited man stopped him mid-sentence and offered his hand. 'Not at all, sir. You must be our new resident. I'm Councillor Fisher.'

He shook his hand. Councillor Fisher had a salesman's voice and exuded a level of confidence that instantly put Philip on the defence. He always trusted his first impressions, and at that moment, he didn't know why, but he didn't like him. Maybe it was Karen's demeanour that made him feel that way, he wasn't sure.

'Philip,' he said, still withholding his last name.

'Very nice to meet you and welcome to our wonderful little town,' Councillor Fisher said.

Karen rolled her eyes.

'Thank you.' Philip said. 'Did you say Councillor Fisher?'

'Yes. I've been the councillor here for over sixteen years now.'

'Really?'

'Yes. I do a good job and I get involved with the people on the ground so I keep getting voted back in. I can't say no and let my voters down, can I?'

'I suppose not.'

Philip wasn't one hundred percent sure a moment ago, but now he was; he didn't like him. He now realised it wasn't a salesman's voice; it was a politician's.

'What can I get you, Philip?' Karen said.

'I bought a fudge cake when I was in this morning but I can't find it.'

For some reason, this sentence caused the two of them to look at each other, only very briefly, but they definitely did.

'Oh yes. I put it back on the shelf,' Karen said before walking from behind the counter and getting the cake. 'I put it back rather than let it go out of date. I'd have replaced it for you next time I saw you.'

'OK, thanks,' Philip said, taking the box from her. 'I thought I'd unpacked it, but I wasn't sure.'

There was an awkward silence as the three of them stood there saying nothing. Philip thought it was time for him to leave. Whatever the problem was between them, he had enough of his own problems to keep him from getting involved.

'Well, I'll leave you to it.'

'Yes. Nice to meet you, Philip,' Councillor Fisher said.

'See you later, Philip,' Karen said. 'Lock your doors.'

Philip left the shop and headed back home.

7

After cutting himself a third of the cake and eating every last crumb from the plate, Philip decided to take a walk to the lighthouse. The snow was falling again and it was fully dark by now. He made his way through the deep snow and off the road, then through the gates that led to the attractive red-bricked building, now in full working order as the light spun its way across the snow-covered bay. The beam of light cut through the falling snow and illuminated a stream of yellow that stretched out as far as Philip could see, starting on the opposite side before quickly dragging across to the left, then starting again at the other side.

Philip walked along the track that led to the door. He was just about to knock when he spotted the intercom on the wall. He pressed the buzzer. Moments later he heard a crackly voice.

'Who's that?'

'Tom, it's Philip.'

'Down in a minute,' he said. The intercom went dead.

Philip stood there shivering for a good three or four minutes before Tom finally opened the door.

'Come on in, Philip,' he shouted. 'What are you doing out in this weather?'

'I wanted to see inside the lighthouse. I've never been in one before.'

Tom looked happy all of a sudden. 'You're in for a treat then. Come on.'

Tom turned to climb the metal spiral staircase, but then he stopped and turned back. 'I have a rule though.'

'What's that?'

'Don't talk until we get to the top. We'll never make it otherwise.'

Philip laughed, but a few minutes of climbing and he began to realise that Tom wasn't joking. The stairs were relentless. He began to wonder how Tom had got down to let him in so fast.

As they finally reached the top of the staircase, Philip was surprised to enter a room that felt like a small flat. There was a kitchen area with a sink and microwave oven. In the centre of the room there was a small dining room table with four chairs, an armchair – where Daisy sat – and a fridge. There was also a window overlooking the sea, about the size of an average kitchen window.

'Tea or coffee?' Tom asked.

'Tea, two sugars please.'

'Feel free to go and enjoy the view before we have our drink,' he said, pointing behind Philip.

Philip turned to see a metal ladder fixed to the wall that led to what looked like a mezzanine balcony. He climbed the ladder – even though his legs were still aching from climbing the staircase – and stepped out onto a floor with windows all the way around. He slowly walked around the narrow floor, taking in the view. The large light spun in the centre, causing him to briefly squint as it hit him. He stood still and looked out over the sea as the stream of light danced by. Now that he was inside a lighthouse for the first time, he was starting to see why Tom would do his best to keep this fantastic building in use. Although it was pitch black, the light lit up the ocean as it spun. He could see the crashing waves of the perilous sea in the stream of light. This was an experience he'd never forget. He hoped it wouldn't be the last time he'd get to stand there.

A few moments later, Tom shouted from the level below, 'Tea's ready.'

Philip climbed back down the ladder and stroked the sleeping dog on the armchair before sitting opposite Tom at the table.

'Well,' Tom said. 'What d'you think of my second home?'

Philip smiled. 'I'm actually quite envious that you get to spend your days here. This is an amazing building.'

'It also serves as my sanctuary.'

'From what?'

'Everyday life.'

'I'm surprised you haven't got a bed here too.'

'It's crossed my mind, but as much as I love being here, I also love my home.'

'Are you married?' Philip asked.

'Widowed.'

'Sorry to hear that. When did that sad day occur?'

Tom took a sip of his tea as he seemed to struggle to remember. 'Four years next month.'

'What would your wife have said about you spending all your time here?'

Tom smiled. 'Most nights she'd bring me some supper, or call at the chippy on her way here. She loved it as much as me.'

Philip let the silence continue as Tom seemed to think about his late wife with a smile on his face.

After another sip of his drink, Tom said, 'So how are you settling in to Greysands?'

'OK so far. I met the councillor this afternoon.'

Tom's smile disappeared.

'I get the feeling that nobody likes him.'

'Did you like him?' Tom asked.

'My first impression wasn't great to be honest.'

'Well keep to that opinion. He'll try his best to get you on his side but believe me, he is a horrible person. He acts like he owns everyone.'

'Really?'

'Yes. And in many cases, you could say that's true.'

'What d'you mean?' Philip asked.

'He acts like he's a self-made millionaire, but he isn't. He inherited everything from his dad. Now his dad was a nice bloke, I had a lot of time for him. But he bought more and more property in this town and unfortunately he left it to his son when he died.'

'What does he own?'

'Most things. My house, Karen's shop, the cafe, pretty much all the commercial buildings in Greysands. He doesn't own the businesses, just the buildings.'

Philip wondered if Tom was suffering the sin of envy. 'Does that make him a bad person?'

'If he just let people get on with things like his dad used to then there wouldn't be a problem. But he doesn't. He throws his weight around and sticks his nose in where it's not wanted.'

'Why do people keep voting him in then?'

Tom laughed.

'He's not really a councillor for Greysands. He's based in Blackpool. Technically the town is under Blackpool's borough, but he acts like he's in some sort of power and does all the communicating for the town. The reason he gets voted in is because nobody at Blackpool cares about this town. And none of the locals would interfere with his election because he owns everything here. He's subtly hinted for many years that while he was the councillor of Greysands then the businesses would get an easy ride.'

'And do they?'

'Easier than if he wasn't voted in. Think about it, Philip; if he wanted to put Karen's rent through the roof, what could she do? Move to another building? He'll only own that one too.'

'There are ombudsmen that stop landlords from doing that,' Philip said.

'That won't make a difference in a place like this, Philip,' Tom said, shaking his head. 'Her only choice would be to move away and set up shop in another town, which is what some residents have done.'

'That shouldn't happen.'

'I know.'

They sat in silence for a moment. Philip didn't like the councillor when he met him, but he didn't think that he was as bad as Tom had just told him. Philip didn't like bullies, but this wasn't his fight. He didn't want to get involved with something where he couldn't see an easy outcome for the locals. Perhaps he wasn't as bad as Tom was making out. His rents might be high, but they couldn't be paying that much, not in a rundown seaside town such as this. There wouldn't be much money going over the counter anyway, and there certainly wouldn't be enough to pay what Philip thought was sounding like a protection racket.

After his drink, he thanked Tom and made his journey back down the many steps and through the snow towards home.

He'd had a reasonably successful first day. He'd met three of the locals, visited a lighthouse and written a good number of pages for his novel.

He was quite happy with his first day in his new home.

8

Philip couldn't sleep. He just lay there thinking about Lesley, wondering what she was doing, what she was thinking, and whether she was any closer to forgiving him. She'd told him when he was begging for her forgiveness that his only chance of them working things out was if he moved away and stayed out of the public eye for a while. She'd said she'd contact him when she was ready to talk, but she couldn't contact him at the moment, even if she did want to.

First thing tomorrow morning Philip was going to organise getting the phone line and an internet connection. Then he would ring Daniel with his new number and get him to pass it on to Lesley. At least he'd know that she could contact him if she wanted to. For all Philip knew at that point, she was wanting to speak to him. He doubted it, but he still wanted to sort the landline out as soon as possible; just in case.

The bedroom was almost completely black as he lay there trying to sleep. The light from the lighthouse shone past the window in the distance, lighting the curtains very slightly, but not enough to disturb him.

He felt his thoughts drift back into his novel, then moments later, he fell asleep.

Philip dreamt about his fictional character, Detective Inspector Lauren Bates. This wasn't unusual. He'd dreamt about her a lot over the years. The usual dream for him was set in the detectives' office. He was watching while all the detectives were arguing about a case. He always tried to chip in with ideas, but they never heard him. Even when he shouted, they just carried on regardless. They occasionally looked at him, but ignored him and quickly continued with their discussion. This was a regular dream for him when working on a novel. He always wanted to consult a dream expert to find out what it meant, but he never did.

During this dream, as the detectives were talking, their voices dropped in volume only to be taken over by a rustling sound. It was a noise Philip didn't recognise. It was almost like a shuffling noise on a wooden floor.

The detectives stopped talking and looked at him. Their expressions were all the same. It was as if they were confused at why he wasn't answering a question, but none of them had asked one.

The rustling became louder and their expressions became more and more confused; some of them shook their heads in disbelief. The noise got too much to ignore in the end and Philip quickly sat up in his bed. He realised that the noise wasn't in his dream, it was in his bedroom.

As the light from the lighthouse shot past the curtains, Philip saw a black figure scurry from the bedroom on all fours through the open door.

'Hey!' he shouted in fear, as he saw the creature leave the room. He wondered if he'd imagined it, but he thought he'd left the door closed, and now it was wide open. He heard the thing scurry down the wooden staircase, making a quiet but high-pitched chattering noise as it went.

Philip's heart was pounding hard in his chest, but he had to do something. He unplugged the lamp from the side of the bed, quickly unscrewed the bulb and removed the lampshade. He ran out onto the landing, holding the lamp like a hammer, ready to hit whatever it was that had invaded his home.

He reached up to the wall just outside of the bedroom and turned the light on before leaning over the banister to see if it was still on the stairs. He couldn't see anything and he couldn't hear anything. He slowly made his way down the stairs, still holding the lamp high, ready to swing. He was terrified, but he had to defend his house. Once at the bottom of the stairs he turned the hallway light on. Still nothing. He checked the front door, confirming it was locked. He walked briskly around the house, turning lights on and checking doors and windows as he went. There was nothing there. He looked through the window at the front of the house. The snow was still falling and there were no new tracks leading to the house. He made his way to the back of the house and looked through the window – it was the same there.

He poured himself a glass of water and stood in the kitchen in his T-shirt and boxer shorts, thinking the only explanation was that he'd dreamt it. It felt very real, and he knew he'd closed the bedroom door. He always closed it at home, and he knew he'd do the same here. But what other explanation was there other than it being a dream? In his mind, he could still see the shadow of the figure as it left his bedroom. It was about the size of a Labrador dog, but there was nothing in the house and the snow outside was untouched. It had to be a dream; there wasn't anything else it could be.

He climbed the stairs and went back to bed. Half an hour or so later, he'd convinced himself it must've been a dream, and drifted back off to sleep.

9

Philip's second day in Greysands wasn't as successful as the first when it came to writing. Every time he sat down, he started to think about the previous night's disturbance. He already thought he'd dreamt it; he even began to wonder if the whole thing had been a dream and he hadn't got out of bed at all. But the lampshade he'd taken off the lamp still lay at the side of the bed, and the glass he'd drank water from was still in the sink that morning when he made his first cup of tea of the day.

He didn't believe in ghosts and he definitely didn't believe in monsters, so what was it? All the doors and windows were locked and there was no disturbance in the snow, other than his own tracks leading up to the front door.

After his third cup of tea, and only seven lines of dialogue, most of which he knew he'd be deleting, he made his way to the phone box outside Karen's shop. The phone company promised to send someone to come and connect a landline and broadband for him. They had no record of ever having a phone at that address and as he looked back at the telegraph poles in the street, he noticed that there wasn't a cable connected to his house. He wondered whether they'd be able to connect him quickly or if he'd be better off finding an electrical shop and buying a cheap mobile phone. He hadn't seen any electrical shops in Greysands, but maybe if the snow cleared, he could travel to Blackpool or Morecambe to buy one. He'd enjoyed the first day without contact to his old life, but already by day two, he wondered whether Lesley wanted to speak to him or not.

On the way back to the house, he decided to call in the cafe that was situated between the pub and the grocery store. As he walked in, he yet again felt as though he'd gone back in time. The small cafe was filled with wooden benches with red leather padding. Each table had a vinegar bottle, salt, pepper and a bottle of ketchup. There was an old man sitting in the window who didn't look up from his newspaper. An old-looking black Labrador lay by his feet.

As Philip reached the counter, a lady came to greet him. She looked around sixty. She was dressed in black trousers and a white blouse, covered by a red apron, with full make-up and perfectly styled short grey hair. She clearly took pride in her appearance. Philip guessed she was the owner.

'Hello there,' she said.

'Good morning,' Philip said. 'I'd like a latte please.'

'Of course, dear,' she said, smiling. 'Anything else?'

The food smelled good and Philip was tempted to order a fry-up, but he opted for something smaller. 'Err ... bacon sandwich, please.'

She scribbled on her pad before saying, 'Four-fifty, please.'

After paying, he went over and sat by the window, at the opposite side of the door to the old man.

After a few moments, the man spoke. Again, he didn't look up from his paper. 'How d'you like your new home?'

This caused Philip to laugh a little. 'Is that going to happen wherever I go in Greysands?'

The man finally looked up. He was eighty-five if he was a day, Philip thought. But he was dressed smartly in a shirt and tie, covered by a V-neck jumper. His long grey coat was on the seat at the side of him.

'What d'you mean?'

'People knowing I'm the new tenant before I tell them.'

The man gave a nod. 'Oh yes. To us who've spent our lives in Greysands, we've seen it all before. You're not the first, and you won't be the last.'

'The last what?'

'The last one to think you can move here and live a normal life.'

Philip was intrigued. 'Why can't I live a normal life?'

The man laughed. 'You'll see.'

'Gerald!' the lady said from behind the counter.

Gerald looked down at his paper again and the lady went back to what she was doing.

Moments later Gerald got up and put his coat on. His dog stood up without having to be told. 'Thanks, Babs,' he shouted.

'Take care, Gerald,' she called back.

Gerald gave a nod to Philip before leaving the cafe.

A few minutes later, Babs brought him his bacon sandwich and coffee.

'Thank you,' Philip said, looking up at her.

She smiled, but Philip didn't think it was genuine. He wondered if she was just busy and had things to do, but at that moment, there was nobody else in the cafe.

'Have you a moment to join me?' Philip said, pointing to the bench opposite him.

'No,' she said. 'Thank you, but I have things to get ready before the rush. Even with the snow, we'll still get the locals in for their dinner.'

'Please,' he said.

She begrudgingly sat down.

Philip offered a hand which she gently shook. 'I'm Philip.'

'Babs,' she said.

Philip took a sip of his coffee, but left the bacon sandwich to one side for now. It didn't bother him if it went cold; in fact, he preferred bacon cold.

'What's going on here?' he asked.

'I don't know what you ...'

Philip politely cut her off. 'You know what I'm getting at. What the old fellow just said, and the fact that I keep getting told to lock my doors.'

Babs looked down at the table and then started messing with her wedding ring, twirling it around her finger.

'I feel like I've moved to a ghost town, which I don't mind, I'd just rather know why people are acting so enigmatic around me.'

'We're a strange little town, that's all,' she said. 'I'm sure you'll get used to us.'

Before Philip could ask any more questions, he saw Babs look over his shoulder towards the front door. Her expression dropped as if she was about to be visited by an unwelcome visitor. Seconds later the door opened.

Philip turned to see the councillor of Greysands walk in. His eyes made contact with Philip's.

'Good day to you, Philip,' he said, offering his hand to be shaken.

Philip obliged.

'And hello to you, Babs. Do us a fry-up, will you?' he said.

Babs got up from the bench without speaking and went back behind the counter.

Philip was displeased to see the councillor take her place and sit opposite him.

'Enjoying Greysands so far?'

'It's a strange little place, but I'm starting to like it.' Philip wondered how much information he should reveal to this man. It was quite obvious that people didn't like him. Philip didn't like him either. But he still wondered if he was as bad as Tom said.

'I'm sure you'll love it once you know your way around.' He pointed to Philip's food. 'Eat. Don't let me stop you.'

Philip picked up his bacon sandwich and took a bite. He decided to see how honest this man was. After swallowing he asked, 'Tell me something; why does a town this size need a councillor?'

'Interesting question, Philip. I'm not officially the councillor for Greysands. Not strictly speaking anyway.'

Perhaps he *was* an honest man, Philip thought.

'No. I began to act in our town's interest when I could see nothing was happening. I'm a councillor for Blackpool really. But we were getting messed about by Blackpool council so I started town meetings in the old church hall, and it grew from there. This town gets ignored and I've been using my contacts at the Blackpool Metropolitan Council to help us.'

'Really?'

'Yes. I'm not always successful, but I give it my best.'

Philip pictured the disused amusement park and algae filled fountains.

'I'll be honest with you Mr Fisher,' Philip said, purposely not calling him by his title. 'I look around this town and I love it. But I love the hidden story behind it, the tragedy, the dark past that screams out at you when you drive through what others might see as a dead town. I know I've not been here long, but I don't see any signs of a successful fight from anyone. The amusement park, the empty shops, the dirty fountains and disused kiddies train track. When you say "not always successful", what examples have you got to show you have won some battles?'

Philip spoke politely, but he could see he'd rattled the councillor's cage as he shifted in his seat, his face reddening.

'The things you mentioned are an ongoing struggle, but there are businesses still thriving in Greysands because of my negotiating power, and they wanted to knock the lighthouse down, but I fought tooth and nail to keep that building in use.'

Philip stared at him, waiting for more, but it looked like Councillor Fisher had finished listing his accomplishments.

'So, if I'm still here by summer, I'll see some improvements?' Philip asked.

'I'm sure you will. The amusement park is probably going to be the last thing to be dealt with, but the others you mentioned; hopefully I'll be making some headway very soon.'

Philip took one last bite of his sandwich before getting up from his seat. 'Well,' he said. 'Nice talking to you Councillor Fisher. I'll look forward to hearing more about your wonderful little town.'

He turned to Babs who was still behind the counter. 'Thanks,' he called.

'OK, love. Take care,' she shouted from the back of the cafe.

Philip left and closed the door behind him, slowly, in case either of them wanted to tell him to lock his doors, but they didn't. He headed home.

10

Philip managed twelve pages, after deleting the work he'd attempted before his trip to the cafe. It was mid-evening, so he decided to go and see Tom in the lighthouse again. Tom had told him to visit any time he wanted, so he put his coat on and left the house.

As he reached the bottom of his path, he looked again towards the beautiful building that was reaching up through the snow and spinning its light across the ocean surrounding the snow-covered town. But as beautiful as it was, he decided to turn left instead of right. He'd call on Tom another time. Tonight, he was going to visit his local pub.

He wouldn't normally drink while in the middle of a novel, but he thought – especially after everything that happened recently – that he'd make an exception and treat himself to a pint of bitter.

He trod his way through the snow to the small row of terraced buildings where the pub was situated. Philip didn't think the pub could be very big inside; it was the same-sized building as the cafe and the shop. But as he walked through the door, he was surprised to see that the room seemed to go further back than the other buildings, making it a decent size; bigger than it looked from the outside at least.

As he walked into the room, which was quite crowded for a pub in such a small town, the noise of all the residents talking and laughing slowly came to a halt as their faces turned to look at him.

There were four tables to the left of the room, but only three on the right side because of the space taken by the burning log fire. There was a crowd of people standing at the bar, many of them dressed as if they were the local fishermen, all with drinks in their hands.

The sudden silence reminded him of *An American Werewolf in London*, when the travellers walked into the pub on the moors to find that everyone suddenly stopped talking and stared at them. That was what he was experiencing now; a sudden silence as the patrons checked out their new neighbour. Philip just stood in the doorway looking back at them, wondering if he was welcome or not. But he was stubborn. His money was as good as anyone else's. Even if he wasn't to be made welcome, he wouldn't be leaving in a hurry. He'd want to know why, or possibly just ignore them and enjoy his drink anyway.

'Welcome to Greysands,' a voice said.

Philip focused on the voice, coming from the barmaid. She was in her mid-to-late thirties, with dark hair in a ponytail, a very pretty smile and gorgeous brown eyes that stayed on him.

'What can I get you?'

Philip was a little blindsided. There were all these people staring at him, and through the crowd he could see a beautiful face that at that moment felt like it belonged to his only friend.

She continued to smile and gave a little nod as if to convince him it was OK to be there.

Philip walked towards the bar and felt for his wallet. 'Pint of your best bitter, please.' His own voice was deafening over the silence of the room.

'Coming right up,' she said, taking a glass from the shelf above her head and then pulling the pump towards her. She seemed a little uncomfortable at the silence as the other patrons continued to stare at him. But she carried on pouring his drink and seemed to try to ignore the awkwardness.

Some of them continued to drink, and some of them stepped aside as Philip made his way to the bar, but still none of them spoke.

Philip began to see the awkwardness as a challenge and tried his best to look as comfortable as he could.

'Three-fifty please,' she said, still smiling.

Philip couldn't remember the last time he'd paid so little for a pint of bitter. After taking his change he turned around to face the room, sipping his bitter as he did, which tasted like a top-quality ale.

He saw a small table next to the door and on the wall was a bookshelf with a collection of very old books residing there. He noticed a copy of *Haunted* by James Herbert and slowly walked over to it, still trying to act as though the silence wasn't bothering him. He took it from the shelf and sat down at the table and opened it at the beginning. He'd read the book some years earlier, and he remembered liking it, so at that moment, he used it to try and help him relax in the pub. By the time he'd reached the bottom of the first page, people had started whispering; by the time he'd finished the first chapter, the room was chattering away like every other pub, and Philip could finally relax and enjoy his pint.

'You like ghost stories then?' he heard a voice ask.

He looked up and saw the barmaid standing at his table with a couple of empty glasses in her hand.

'I prefer crime, but I read this a while ago. I remember enjoying it, and I didn't guess the ending. That's always a good thing.'

'Really?' she said. 'I like to try and guess the ending when I read a book.'

'Oh, me too,' Philip said. 'But I'm disappointed if I guess right, or even worse, if my ending is better than the author's. I feel let down if that happens.'

'Oh, I see. You like to be surprised?'

'I do.'

She stood for a moment smiling at him.

He smiled back at her, wondering if their conversation was over, or just beginning.

'I'm Charlotte.'

'Philip,' he said, offering his hand. 'Nice to meet you.'

'You too.'

'What kind of books do you like to read?' he asked.

'I like crime fiction too. But anything in that genre I'll give a try,' she said, pointing to the book.

'You're a fan of horror?'

'Yes. I love it when the power goes out and I have to read a creepy ghost story by candlelight.'

'You said that as if the power goes out a lot,' Philip said.

'At least once a week,' she said, smiling.

'Really?'

'Yes. It's quite a common thing here.'

'What causes that to happen?'

Charlotte seemed to think for a moment, almost as if she was so used to the power going out that she'd never questioned it before.

'I don't know. Maybe because we're miles from any other

town, or maybe the lighthouse causes a fuse to blow.'

Philip smiled. 'Maybe.'

She looked back towards the bar before saying, 'I'd better get back to work, but nice talking to you, and welcome to the town.'

As Philip watched her walk away, he wondered why his heart jumped a little. He was in a strange town, far away from home, and he should be missing his wife and trying to think of how to get her back. But instead, he was wondering if he'd get a chance to know Charlotte a little more.

She was definitely in her mid-thirties, he thought, so she was far too young for him. Although he enjoyed flirting with younger ladies, he didn't consider himself handsome enough to get serious interest from a lady so much younger than him. He'd had many offers from ladies in the past, but was it just that he was rich and reasonably famous, or did he have a certain charm that they liked? He was sure that nobody knew who he was in Greysands, and he wanted to keep it that way. So maybe Charlotte did find him interesting. He certainly found her interesting.

She was beautiful – not model-beautiful, but very naturally pretty. She wore very little make-up and was dressed casually in jeans and a white T-shirt. Philip wanted to talk to her some more. But he thought that he might have to leave it for another night. For all he knew, she was spoken for, and he didn't want to upset the locals by showing an obvious interest in her. For now, he had to play it cool. And he really should be thinking of ways to fix his marriage, not how to make a move on a lady he'd just met.

He decided to stay for another pint, but after that one, he

said a quick goodbye to Charlotte and made his way home. He didn't want to scare her by appearing too eager. But he definitely thought that this was the first of many evenings in this pub.

11

Philip walked around his house checking everywhere thoroughly before calling it a night. He was wearing a T-shirt and pyjama bottoms. The old house was too big and too cold to walk around dressed like this, he thought. He did bring a dressing gown, but he only usually wore it when getting out of the shower. He wished he'd brought the reindeer onesie that Lesley bought him for Christmas as a joke, only to discover that it was the warmest and most comfortable item of clothing he owned.

He was very security conscious anyway, but since the event of the previous night, he thought he'd better double-check everywhere before he let his head hit the pillow. Every window was shut and every door was locked. He looked out of the front window to try and make a mental note of the tracks in the snow that led up to the door. The snow at the back of the house was undisturbed, and Philip hoped it would stay that way. The amusement park was also covered by a blanket of white that still lay untouched.

Philip thought about the conversation he had with Charlotte about the power going out. He thought he'd better look around for any candles and if he couldn't find any, he'd better get some from Karen's. If the power going out was a regular thing, then surely she kept a decent amount in stock. But sure enough, he found some in the bottom drawer in the kitchen. There were at least twenty white candles lying loose, some of them used and reduced to half their size. This made Philip think – in the deductive manner of DI Lauren Bates – that the power probably stayed off for an hour or so at a time. There were also several boxes of matches in the drawer.

He took a couple of the candles and one box of matches out, carried them through to the living room and placed them in the desk drawer. If the power went out, he'd most likely be either in bed or at his desk working. So he thought the drawer was a good place to keep some.

After turning off all the lights, he climbed the stairs, brushed his teeth, and then climbed into his bed.

Insomnia wasn't something he usually suffered with, but tonight he struggled to switch off. He thought about Lesley and how he missed her. But if he really missed her that much, why would he be so interested in Charlotte? Maybe it was time to let go and move on. He was finding Greysands to be a strange town, with secrets that he hadn't yet discovered. But he also found it an interesting place with interesting people.

He was also struggling to sleep because of the – possibly imaginary – intruder from the previous night. Every little creek that the tired old house gave caused him to sit up and listen for more noises.

It felt like an eternity before he fell asleep. He didn't know what time it was, but he guessed it to be at least three, possibly three-thirty. He was getting himself worked up at the thought of a wasted writing day. He didn't function very well without his full quota of sleep, and so knew that the next day wouldn't be successful as far as writing was concerned.

Finally, when he'd pushed aside his frustration, and the fear of creatures wandering around his house, he drifted peacefully off to sleep.

12

The loud banging noise made Philip jump up and quickly look around the bedroom. He expected to see something scurrying about, but there was nothing there, and his door was closed. The winter sun shone low through the curtains, lighting the room a little. He reached over to the bedside table and picked up his watch. It was ten-thirty. He couldn't remember the last time he'd slept in so late.

He heard a banging once more and realised that it was someone knocking on the front door. He went over to the window and looked through the curtains to see a van parked on the main road and a man in a hard hat climbing out of it. When Philip looked down, he saw another man standing on his path. He knocked on the window and waved to him before going down to open the door, straightening his hair as he went.

'Mr Lloyd?' the man asked. He was dressed like a builder but he also wore a high visibility jacket.

'Yes.'

'We're here to install your phone line.'

'That was quick. Come in.'

'No, sir,' he said. 'Most of what we've got to do is out here. We'll knock when we've got to come inside, all right?'

'Don't knock,' Philip said. 'Just come in. I had a sleepless night last night. Sorry if I didn't hear you first time.'

'No problem.'

As the man walked back to his van, he passed a lady on

Philip's path, heading towards the house. She was wearing a long winter coat and a woollen hat, and carrying a white plastic carrier bag.

When Philip saw her smile, he realised who it was.

'Good morning,' she said.

'Good morning, Charlotte. What brings you here?'

'I've brought you some breakfast,' she said, holding up the carrier bag.

'Really?'

Charlotte nodded, still smiling.

'That's very kind of you. Come in,' he said, standing aside.

Charlotte's smile disappeared. 'No. It's OK. I just thought I'd bring you some breakfast, as a welcome to the town, and as an apology for the not-so-friendly welcome from the rest of the folk in the pub.'

'No need,' he said. 'Come inside.'

'No really,' she said.

Philip was confused. 'Charlotte, come in. I'll make us a cup of tea. I'll be making the workmen one anyway.'

Charlotte looked around, seeming a little anxious.

'You can trust me, I'm a perfect gentleman.' *Not counting recent events, that is,* he thought.

'OK,' she said, and stepped into the house.

Philip made them a cup of tea, and one each for the telephone engineers, and took them out to them. When he came back in, he sat at the kitchen table opposite Charlotte.

'It's just a sausage sandwich; is that OK?'

'Perfect,' he said. 'Are you not eating?'

'I ate at the cafe.'

'I see.'

He took a bite of his sandwich. It had already gone cold in the short walk from the cafe to his house, but this didn't bother him. He was still taken aback by the gesture.

'So, what have I done to deserve this treatment?'

'It's just my way of welcoming you to Greysands.'

'Well, that's very kind of you,' he said before taking another bite.

'What are the workmen doing?' she asked.

'Installing a phone line.'

'Don't you have a mobile phone?'

'No. And I don't ever plan on getting one.'

She laughed. 'You're probably the only person in the world without one.'

'So I'm told. I'm happy just having a land line and the answer service. I just need to find somewhere that sells phones. Is there somewhere in town where I can buy one?'

'I'll bring you one.'

'Really?'

'Yes. I'll have a spare one somewhere. I'll dig it out and bring it around for you.'

'Thank you.'

Charlotte, as nice as she was being, was still a little on edge for some reason. She didn't seem nervous when he spoke to her in the pub, and she looked quite confident when she walked up his path. But she was definitely uncomfortable now, Philip thought.

'So, how are you enjoying your new house?' she asked.

'It's perfect,' he said.

'Perfect?'

His answer seemed to surprise her.

'Yes. I love the house, and so far, I'm quite happy with the town. You seemed surprised. Shouldn't I be enjoying it?'

She shifted in her seat. 'Err ... no. I mean yes. Greysands is a great little town. And the house is ...' She seemed to struggle to finish the sentence.

'Old and dingy?' Philip said.

Charlotte laughed. 'I wasn't going to say that.'

'It is, though,' Philip said. 'But it's perfect for me.'

'Why's that?'

Philip didn't want to give away who he was. He still wasn't sure if the video of him and Jade Romily had been released to the public or not. The longer he could keep his identity to himself the better. He certainly didn't want the locals of Greysands to know who he was if the newspapers got a hold of the story of his infidelity.

'I work from home, and the view of the sea through the window is amazing. It's very therapeutic.'

'It is that,' she said.

'Tell me something,' Philip started. 'An old chap in the cafe – I think his name was Gerald – he gave me the impression that I wouldn't last in this town. Is there a reason for him saying that?'

'Oh, don't take any notice of Gerald. He lives in a world of his own. That'll be him just trying to frighten you.'

'Why would he want to frighten me?'

Charlotte looked at her watch. 'I could do with making a move. I have a lot to do today before I start my shift at the pub.'

Philip was thinking that yet again, he'd had a conversation with a local who was trying to keep something from him.

'Charlotte,' Philip said.

She had started to stand up but stopped as Philip said

her name.

'Is there something going on that I need to know?'

She didn't move for a moment as she seemed to think about what to say. She then obviously thought better of it. 'I don't know what you mean,' she said before standing up and pushing the chair back under the table.

'OK,' he said.

Philip wasn't ready to give up on Charlotte, but he felt that taking it slowly might be the best way to find out what was going on. She might be someone who would be his friend and possibly confide in him whatever secrets Greysands had. He didn't want to scare her away by putting too much pressure on her.

'Will I see you in the pub later?' she said as she walked away.

'I'm sure you will,' Philip said.

'Bye for now,' she said as she left the house, followed by, 'Lock your doors.'

He didn't know what to think. There was something not quite right about Greysands. He didn't know if it was something to do with the house he was in, or maybe even the creature that interrupted his sleep the night before last. But he knew for sure that it was something to do with the councillor.

He finished his breakfast, and got himself showered while the engineers installed his phone line. After that, he settled down in his chair in front of the window and spent most of the day writing.

13

Every now and then, Philip would experience an overload of energy and concentration that would lead him to do an incredible amount of work in just one sitting. He remembered his third Lauren Bates novel, *Return Ticket*; that was the first time it happened.

Some writers plan everything out in great detail before they start to write; others just go by the seat of their pants and see where the story takes them. Philip was somewhere in between. He made notes as he went along with his first draft and planned it out thoroughly for his second. During *Return Ticket*, he'd made many pages of notes before typing the first word. He'd cut out pieces of paper and wrote each scene out before laying them across his dining room table. Then, after jotting down all the scenes into his note pad, he began to write.

The story was going reasonably well for the first week or so, but once he'd reached one hundred and sixty-two pages, he got stuck. It just wasn't working. He'd kept to his notes, but he just wasn't feeling the enthusiasm for the story that he normally felt.

It was just past nine-thirty at night when he put his note pad back in the drawer, made himself a cup of tea, and then continued to write. He decided to ignore the list of scenes and just go where the story wanted to go. He remembered a famous author once saying that as a writer, you're not so much writing the story as you are the first reader. That was how he felt as the story went into places he couldn't have imagined. He wrote without censoring himself and this led to some very graphic and violent scenes, which helped towards the book's success.

He would normally write for about three hours or so, but that night he just kept going. The 250-page novel was finished that night. He'd written from page 162, all the way to the end. It was only the first draft and he knew it would need several more months of work before it was ready for his publisher, but he was amazed that he could do so much work in one night.

Philip remembered the strange sensation of realising that there was light coming through the curtains and looking at the clock to find just how long he'd been working. That novel would always be his favourite. He'd never managed to do an all-night session since that night. He'd tried but he'd never got past three in the morning, but now he felt that today's session was coming close. The sausage sandwich that Charlotte had brought him was the only thing he'd had to eat that day. He'd stopped for several cups of tea, but he didn't stop for any more food.

He scrolled back through his work. He was on page forty-five at the start of the day. He was now on page eighty-seven. Forty-two pages was a very good day's work, he thought. Not as good as the sleepless night all those years ago, but it was still a very successful day.

He wondered if he should just keep going but his eyes were getting heavy and his stomach was rumbling. He was also starting to make more and more spelling mistakes. He always used to say to Lesley, *When you're pushing delete more than any other key, it's time to stop for the day.*

He stretched and rubbed his eyes when suddenly a bang made him jump. It wasn't too loud, but it was loud enough to make his heart pump harder than it had all day, as he tried to work out what it was. He looked around the room. After a second or two he realised that the lamp wasn't on. He then turned back to his laptop to find that the screen had dimmed a little from its usual level of brightness.

The power had gone out.

He saved his work and then turned off the laptop.

After taking a candle out of his desk drawer and lighting it, he went to the kitchen and took a small plate from the cupboard. He tilted the candle to drip wax onto the plate before balancing it in the tacky white puddle. Once the candle was fixed in place, he then went upstairs, washed his face and changed his clothes. He wondered if the pub could still serve beer in the middle of a power cut. It shouldn't be out for long though, he thought. But he'd told Charlotte that he'd go to the pub, and that's what he was going to do.

While there, he thought that maybe he could find out a little more about this strange little seaside town.

14

When Philip first met Charlotte, he thought of her as pretty. Now, looking at her face by candlelight, he thought of her as beautiful. This started to frighten him a little, but on the other hand, he was excited at the thought of getting to know a lady other than Lesley.

He still loved Lesley and hoped they could fix their marriage, but he found himself caring a little less about getting her back as each day passed. He knew he shouldn't consider himself single at the moment. Lesley asked him to take some time away from her, but she didn't mean he could go and meet other ladies and try to start new relationships. But Philip was miles from his wife, his home and his old life.

He'd even started to feel as though he was miles away from his career. He was writing as well as ever, but hardly a day would pass where he wasn't being asked to do appearances, or interviews, or having to give an answer to a question on his many social media platforms. He never even looked at those pages, but he still had to comment on world events, politics, and especially the death of a famous person. But being here in Greysands, a town that felt as though it was decades behind the rest of the world, Philip felt as though he was free to do as he wanted.

The pub was just as full as it was the previous night. It looked especially cosy with all the candles lit. This made him think that maybe the pub should always trade without power. It might be a good idea for a business, he thought; a candlelit pub.

Nobody paid Philip any attention as he walked up to the bar and ordered a drink from Charlotte. There was no uncomfortable silence, or staring from the fishermen or the other locals as they continued with their conversations.

'Pint of bitter please, Charlotte.'

'Coming right up,' she said, taking a glass from the shelf above the bar. 'I've got that phone for you,' she said.

'Thank you very much,' Philip said. He momentarily wondered if he was better off without it. But he knew that sooner or later he would have to contact his agent and Lesley. So, he thought he'd better take it home with him.

After exchanging a few pleasantries with Charlotte, he sat back at the table from the previous night and took the copy of *Haunted* off the bookshelf again. He found his page and continued to read the story, tilting the book towards the candle on the table.

He'd reached the bottom of his glass and read another thirty pages or so when he heard a voice.

'Mind if I join you?'

Philip looked up to see Tom standing there with two pints of bitter in his hands. Daisy, his whippet stood next to him with her lead trailing along the ground.

Philip closed the book. 'Of course, Tom; take a seat.'

Tom put the drinks on the table and slid one towards Philip. 'There you go,' he said. 'I presume you're not driving home.'

Philip laughed. 'No, I'll think I'll brave the walk.'

'How are things going?' Tom said, after taking a large gulp of his bitter.

'Can't complain.'

'Have you been chatting to any more locals?'

'Just Charlotte. She seems nice. She's giving me a phone.'

'Is she?' Tom said. 'Is that to get in touch with whatever or whoever you're running away from?'

Philip was taken aback by this question. So far, nobody, including Tom, had asked him anything personal. Philip wondered if this conversation was heading that way.

'I'm not prying, Philip. You don't have to tell me anything. But it's obvious you're running away from something. You wouldn't have moved here on your own if not.'

'I suppose.'

Tom was right. Philip was running away. He was running away from a huge mistake. He was running away from a horrible situation that could've easily been avoided. He could've blamed alcohol. Alcohol definitely played a part in the situation. But now, less than a week since he last saw his wife, he was finding his attention being stolen by a lovely young barmaid. Was he guilty of a stupid mistake? Or was he subconsciously sabotaging his marriage so he could start again?

In many ways he and Lesley were happily married. They never argued; they had a clean and tidy house; they had a healthy lifestyle, balancing work and pleasure. They went out for meals with friends weekly, sometimes twice a week. But they hadn't gone out for a meal, just the two of them, in a long time. There were a few things they hadn't done together in a while.

Lesley giving up work and becoming his PA had certainly helped Philip's career, but he was now looking back at the last ten years of his life as a business arrangement.

Sex was one thing missing from their relationship, but so was holding hands, and sharing the odd kiss or hug. And he couldn't remember the last time the word 'love' was used between them.

In the last year or so, Lesley had been spending more and more time out of the house. She always left the house saying, *'I'll get out of your way,'* or *'I'll give you some writing time.'* Their house was huge. She didn't have to go out to give him some peace and quiet. She could throw a party at one end of the house while Philip worked at the other end and he wouldn't hear a thing. They'd definitely been growing apart. He thought maybe he would phone her tomorrow; to let her know his phone number more than anything. But he also wondered if she'd been sent the video, and if she had been sent it, had she watched it? He hoped to God that Jade Romily hadn't sent it to the newspapers or released it onto the Internet.

He knew he'd made the right choice by not paying her, but he also knew that his marriage and career hung in the balance. At that moment, if he had to choose between his marriage and his career, he would choose his career. He was confused at how he didn't seem to care as much as he should about Lesley taking him back. He was going to have to do some serious thinking. He wondered if he was just feeling as though he was in some kind of holiday mode, and after a week or so he'd start to miss home and maybe even miss Lesley. He didn't know.

'Are you happy you chose Greysands to escape to?' Tom said.

Philip took a gulp of his bitter. 'I am,' he said. 'It's an interesting place.'

Tom sniggered. 'Give it time. You won't feel like that after a month or so.'

'I'm not so sure,' Philip said. 'It's a beautiful seaside town. It's got an interesting story hidden away that nobody is sharing at the moment. And an amazing lighthouse right outside my window.'

'That bit's true.'

'Oh. And the power goes out on a regular basis and nobody knows why.'

'It makes for a nice atmosphere though, don't you think?' Tom said, looking around at the candlelit pub.

'It does.'

Philip leaned over the table to Tom. He wanted to know more about the town and the people who lived there. He thought that maybe Tom would give him a little more information about the strange things he'd been experiencing. He decided to start with the local motto.

'Why do people keep telling me to lock my doors?' he whispered.

Tom immediately looked uncomfortable and looked over his shoulder before turning back to face Philip.

'I told you,' he said. 'It's just a saying we have.'

'Tom,' Philip said. He stared into Tom's eyes and waited for a better answer.

Tom shifted uncomfortably in his seat again before answering. 'It's just ...'

Philip waited.

'It's just that the people of this town are a little safety conscious, that's all.'

Philip was disappointed with Tom's response. He wasn't going to argue with the man who was so far the only local to buy him a drink, but he did decide to press a little more in the hope Tom would reveal something to him.

'I come from Manchester, Tom. I always lock my doors, even

when I'm just putting the bin out. So, come on. Why is it so important that I lock my doors here?'

Tom scratched his bald head and quickly looked around the room once more. He then leaned back on the table and looked Philip in the eye with a serious expression that Philip hadn't seen as yet.

'It's just that ...'

'Yeah,' Philip prompted.

'Things aren't always safe around here.'

Philip listened for more.

'It's not the seaside haven you were hoping it to be.'

'In what way?'

'Well ... you might experience strange goings-on in that house.'

'I have already,' Philip said.

He wasn't sure that the intruder two nights earlier had been real or whether he'd imagined the whole thing. But he thought he'd tell Tom and see what he made of it.

'What's happened? Tom asked.

'I woke up to something in my bedroom.'

Tom didn't look surprised.

'I don't know what it was, whether it was human or an animal. I chased it off but I couldn't catch it and I don't know where it went.'

'Hmm,' Tom muttered. 'I told you to lock your doors.'

'I did.'

'You can't have done,' Tom said.

'Trust me. I checked every window and every door. They were all secure.'

'Has anything gone missing?'

'No,' Philip said. He then remembered the cake. 'Actually, I was sure I bought a chocolate cake from Karen. When I came to eat it, I couldn't find it. Karen said I'd left it there and she gave me another one. But I wasn't sure she was telling the truth.'

'And this thing you chased,' Tom said. 'Where did you see it, your bedroom did you say?'

'Yes, my bedroom, but it was dark. I couldn't see it properly. I quickly took the lamp apart so I had a weapon. By the time I got to the landing it was downstairs. By then I could still hear it, but I couldn't see it.'

'And you're certain that all the windows and doors were shut and locked?'

'Positive.'

Suddenly, the pub lit up as the power came back on. It made everyone jump, Philip especially.

When Philip looked around the room, he noticed that some of the locals were looking his way. Tom seemed to notice too and looked a little nervous; his face flushed and he looked down at his drink. He took a large gulp of beer.

Philip realised that they must've been talking loudly. The locals seemed to have been listening to their every word.

'Anyway,' Tom said. 'I'll catch up with you later.' He then stood up and took a hold of Daisy's lead and left the pub.

'Thanks for the drink,' Philip said, but Tom was halfway through the door before he'd finished his sentence.

Philip wasn't sure why Tom had hurried away. He wasn't sure if the locals were unhappy with what they'd heard or if they were intrigued themselves. They looked menacing as they stared. They might've frightened Tom away, but they weren't going to frighten Philip. He stared right back at them. Of all the people who were in the pub, there were only five or six of them looking at him. They were all men aged between thirty and fifty and looked reasonably fit. Philip thought they were fishermen by the way they were dressed, and by the fact that they were all red-faced from working outdoors in rough weather. He knew he couldn't win against them all if it turned violent, but that didn't mean he was going to be intimidated by them.

'It's not as cosy with the power on,' Philip said. It wasn't a very tough line to deliver to a group of men who were staring at him, but he delivered it with confidence. They all turned away and continued with their own conversations.

Philip went back to his drink and opened his book again. He didn't really concentrate on the story; his mind was elsewhere. He thought that tomorrow afternoon would be a good time to climb the lighthouse steps once more.

15

Philip chatted briefly with Charlotte before leaving the pub. He carried the plastic carrier bag containing the phone she gave him as he walked home through the snow. He half expected it to be an old-fashioned rotary telephone with the wheel of numbers that everyone used to have. Everything else about this town seemed several decades behind the rest of the world, so he was surprised when he opened the bag a saw a digital cordless phone with a separate base unit.

Once home, he plugged the phone in and connected the wire to the wall-socket. He felt relief that the phone worked when he heard the tone, but he also felt a little disappointed that the barrier from his old life had now been removed.

It was getting late. But he knew his agent would be up, so he typed his number in to his new phone. After ringing half a dozen times, it went to the answer service.

'Hi Daniel,' he said, holding the piece of paper with his number on. 'This is my new phone number…' Philip read it out. 'Give me a call when you get a chance. Cheers.'

As he sat on the sofa in front of the fire, he thought about the situation he was in. The last few days, even though they were very strange in many ways, were a welcome relief from his old life. He knew he should be happy about talking to Lesley, but he wasn't. What he was really hoping for was to get to know Charlotte a little more. He wondered if he was being stupid. He was very aware of the age gap, but he was also aware of how she looked at him when she spoke. After the incident with Jade Romily, Philip knew he should be keeping away from women. But there was something innocent about Charlotte; something that made him feel as though she was reaching out to him. She hadn't spoken very much as yet, other than to ask him how he was and, of course, to welcome him to Greysands. But the strange way she acted when she came to his house made him feel as though she had something on her mind. He hoped he could get a little more from her. Maybe she would bring him breakfast again, he thought.

He could feel himself drifting off to sleep as he stared at the fire. Why not? He usually preferred to sleep in a bed, but this leather sofa was so comfortable, and the heat from the fire was soothing. He drifted off into a deep sleep.

The clock on the wall in the alcove said three-thirty, or at least he thought it did. The fire had died out and the cold of the room had awoken him. He rubbed his eyes as he sat up before reading the clock again. It was three-twenty-five. He stretched his arms and gave a loud yawn that might've woken his neighbours, had he had any.

He climbed the creaky stairs and made his way to bed. He went into the bathroom to use the lavatory first. As he flushed the chain, he heard a noise outside of the open door. He thought he saw something run past the doorway from the corner of his eye. He quickly looked around the bathroom for a weapon. The only thing he could find was a can of deodorant. He didn't know if this was to spray or throw at his intruder, but it was all he could find that would be remotely useful.

He stepped through the bathroom door and looked around

the dark landing. He couldn't see anything, or anyone. His heart was bouncing around his chest but he couldn't shy away from whatever it was. He momentarily thought of locking himself in the bathroom, but that wasn't his style. He always faced things head on and that's what he was going to do now. Maybe moving to Greysands was running away, but it was Lesley that told him to move somewhere quiet and get away from his past. But other than his recent *emigration*, as Tom put it, running away wasn't something he'd ever done before and he wasn't going to get into the habit of now.

He walked further onto the landing, but couldn't hear any more noises. He leaned over the bannister, like he had the last time he'd been sure he had an intruder in the house. He still couldn't see anything. There were no lights on downstairs. He started to make his way down, one step at a time, his heart still pounding hard. The light switch was on the other side of the landing, but instead of going over and switching it on, he thought he'd try and sneak up on whoever or whatever it was.

Philip continued down the staircase in the dark, still with the can of deodorant in his hand. As he almost reached the bottom, he found he could see a little; the living room was open and the street light outside allowed a small amount of light through the window. But the hallway was still pretty dark. He crouched as he walked, trying to see into the downstairs hallway.

As he got to the last third of the stairs, a sudden, loud, screeching noise filled his ears from behind. As he jumped and turned to look, he stumbled, falling backwards. His head hit the wall as he fell; he rolled down the last few steps to the floor, and as he did, he felt something rush past him, screeching as it went by.

As his face hit the floor, he caught a blurry vision of something moving away in the shadows, running away from the front door and towards the kitchen as the can of deodorant rolled by. It ran fast, like a shadow caused by a moving car. Philip couldn't lift his head to focus. He felt scared and sick. What was in his house? All he could think as he slipped into unconsciousness, was if he'd hurt himself badly, how long would it be before somebody found him?

16

Philip could hear a strange noise. It was a chirpy computerised noise, beeps coming from somewhere in a sporadic array that didn't quite make a tune. His head was pounding, like he had the hangover of all hangovers. But he knew it wasn't drink. He knew he'd been having very strange dreams, but as he tried to open his eyes, he couldn't quite remember what they were.

The beeping noises suddenly stopped, and he found himself fully awake. As he moved, the floor felt cold, apart from the small warm area his face had created. It also felt hard under his face, and he tried to make sense of where he was.

As the sideways view of the open kitchen door came into focus, he instantly remembered everything. The beeping noise must've been his new phone. He hadn't heard the ringtone yet. He realised he was lying at the bottom of the stairs because he'd fallen down them. And the reason he'd fallen down the stairs was because of an intruder, an intruder that pushed by him, sending him flying into the wall before he rolled to the bottom.

Philip sat up and gave himself the once over. He couldn't see or feel anything broken but his head hurt and the left side of his face felt as though he'd taken a blow from a professional boxer. He dragged himself to his feet but he felt dizzy, and sick, so he sat on the stairs while he came around.

He then remembered that it was around three-thirty when he went to bed. If it was the new phone he'd heard ringing, then it must be at least eight in the morning. Four and a half hours was a long time to be lying unconscious at the foot of the stairs. He'd been knocked out before, when he was a police officer. The first time was during a riot outside of a football stadium. Someone punched him full in the face as he was looking the other way. He only knew what had happened because two other officers pounced on the man and arrested him. They filled Philip in on what happened after he came around.

The second time was when he was the passenger in a high-speed chase. The police car rolled as it came off the road. All Philip could remember was the car sliding onto the grass and hitting a wall. Next thing, the car was on its side and people were calling his name. The nauseating feeling of coming back into consciousness was something he could remember all too well. But now, he tried his best to shake it off because for all he knew, whatever it was that caused him to fall down the stairs was still in the house.

He staggered to his feet and negotiated his way through the hallway that seemed to him to have walls that wouldn't keep still. As he reached the kitchen, he had a quick look around to make sure it was empty. Then he went over to the sink to pour himself a glass of water. He hoped this would deal with his thirst and his headache. It quickly cured the first, but not the latter.

He put down the glass and stumbled over to the back door. It was locked. He then checked the windows; they too were locked. He looked through the frosted glass at the untouched snow at the back of his house. This felt as though it was becoming a regular thing for him; chasing an intruder only to find the doors locked and no traces in the snow of their escape.

Did they fly in and out? And if they did, they must have a key.

He walked back through to the front door, then he checked upstairs and as before, nothing. No signs of anyone being in his house.

Was he imagining the whole thing? He'd read about people having nervous breakdowns, but other than his night-time disturbances, he felt perfectly fine. Yes, he'd split up with his wife, and he'd been the victim of attempted extortion, but moving to Greysands was all the therapy he needed. His new friend Tom, and of course Charlotte, were both making him feel at home. This town was definitely set in a time decades ago, but that was fine by him. He felt as though he was back in the eighties, and he loved it.

Maybe he was in a disused town where all the residents had died and everybody he'd spoken to so far were ghosts. He laughed to himself as he thought this, but then he wondered if it was possible. Had he actually touched any of his new acquaintances yet? Yes, of course. He'd shaken hands with Tom, and the councillor. So that theory wasn't looking likely.

He tried to think what this creature was that had disturbed him. Maybe it was time to pin down Tom, or Charlotte, or the councillor, and ask for the truth on what was happening in this town. But first, he felt as though he needed more sleep.

He walked back into the kitchen to make a cup of tea. Even the noise of the water hitting the steel inside of the kettle caused the pounding in his head to increase. After making the cup of tea, he stumbled through to the living room, where the sofa looked even more comfortable than it did the previous night. But before he could fall onto it, the stupid beeping sounds started again.

He answered the phone and sat hunched over at his desk in front of the window, where the curtains were still drawn.

'Hello,' he said, in a croaky voice.

'Philip? Is that you?'

'Yes,' he answered, just as croaky. He coughed to clear his throat. 'Daniel, it's me,' he said.

'Good God, Philip; you sound terrible. Have you got a hangover?'

He wasn't in the mood for a conversation, even though he was wondering how Lesley was, and if the news of his indiscretion had come out yet. 'I haven't, but I feel as though I have.'

'Why, what's wrong?' Daniel asked.

Philip briefly considered telling him the truth about the creature or creatures he'd encountered or imagined in his house. But he thought better of it, for now at least.

'I fell down the stairs. I've been lying unconscious for about three or four hours.'

'Bloody hell, Philip. You need to go to hospital.'

'No. I'm fine. I just need to drink my cup of tea and then get some rest.'

'Look, I'm supposed to be meeting a new client today, but I'll put her off and come and see you. I can take you to hospital. I'll be there within the hour.'

'No,' Philip barked. 'Sorry, no. It's OK, Daniel, honestly. I just need a bit of rest.'

'Look, you sound awful, and being out of it for so long can't be good. You should see a doctor.'

Philip really didn't want Daniel to go out of his way for him, but he also didn't want anyone from his old life visiting him in his new one; not yet anyway.

'Daniel, please, I just want to rest. You see this new client and I'll phone you later once I'm feeling better. OK?'

'OK,' Daniel said.

There was a moment's pause where Philip wanted to ask Daniel if he'd spoken to Lesley. But his head hurt so much that he didn't ask. He didn't want any new information about what Lesley had been up to, or what she was planning for her future, and if it involved Philip, spinning around his head. He needed to sleep.

'I'll speak to you later,' Philip said. 'Thanks for ringing.'

'OK. Take care.'

Philip hung up and took a couple of gulps of tea, then set it down on the coffee table and crashed onto the sofa. He drifted off to sleep within seconds of landing. His head still hurt in his dreams, but not quite as much as when he was awake.

17

Philip woke up and looked around the room. He could see light shining through the gaps in the curtains. His head still hurt as he looked at the clock, but not as much as before. It was just before two o'clock. Maybe he should be worried. He'd slept for several hours on the floor, and now he'd slept – without stirring – for another six hours. Perhaps he was more hurt than he'd first thought.

As he opened the curtains, he saw Charlotte walking along the path to his house.

She saw him and waved.

The light hurt the backs of his eyes, but he thought he'd try to fight the pain and get on with his day. The idea of writing made him feel sick. As addicted to writing as he still was after all these years, he couldn't bring himself to stare at the laptop screen if ever he felt ill, and boy did he feel ill now? But still, as sickly as he felt, seeing Charlotte made him feel a little better.

He went to the front door and let her in; her beautiful face quickly changed from looking as happy as always, to an expression of shock. 'Oh my God, Philip,' she said. 'What happened?'

'I look that bad, eh?' he asked.

'You look like you've been in an accident.'

'Come in and I'll tell you all about it.'

He closed the door and led her through to the kitchen to make them a cup of tea. As he stumbled, Charlotte sat him down at the small kitchen table and took over.

'You stay still,' she said. 'I'll make the drinks. Tea is it?'

'Yeah, two sugars,' he said, rubbing his temples.

'I think you need three. You look terrible. Actually, go through and sit on the sofa. I'll bring the drinks in when they're ready.'

It was hard work standing up again, but he did as he was told.

What felt like only a few minutes later, Charlotte was standing over him, calling his name.

Philip opened his eyes and saw her standing there with a cup of tea in her hand.

'Sorry,' he said. 'I must've drifted off again.'

'Look, Philip, I don't know what's happened, but I've run you a bath. If you don't feel better after that I'll take you to hospital.'

He took a sip of his tea. 'Thanks. I don't need hospital, but the bath might wake me up. I'll go and get in and I'll tell you what happened when I come back down. Will you still be here?'

She looked a little nervous at this question, but nodded anyway. 'Just don't fall asleep in the bath.'

'I won't.'

The bath was enough to make him feel better. It was way too hot but he'd got in anyway, hoping it would shock him into snapping out of whatever it was he was feeling, which it did.

When he walked downstairs in his dressing-gown, feeling much fresher now he'd bathed and brushed his teeth, he saw Charlotte wandering around the living room with a duster in her hand. She'd given the living room a really good spring clean.

'Feeling better?' she asked.

'Much better, thank you. You didn't have to do my housework.'

'It's fine,' she said. 'I've made another cuppa, and some

toast.' She then walked through the living room to the kitchen. 'Come on.'

Philip sat down at the table. He had a quick sip of tea before taking a bite of toast. He thought that maybe this was the perfect time to interrogate Charlotte on what was actually happening in Greysands, but he knew that first she'd want to know how he'd got in such a state.

'So, what happened?' she asked.

He paused for a moment. He wanted to tell her about the creature, but he also wanted to gauge her reaction.

'I was pushed down the stairs,' he said.

Her eyes widened. 'Where?'

'Here,' he said. His police training was coming back to him. Say as little as possible to see if the person you're interrogating gives away any knowledge they already have on the matter.

'Who by?' she asked.

'I don't know.'

The silence seemed to continue forever.

Finally, Charlotte said, 'You're not making sense.'

'No?'

'Well, who was in the house with you?'

'Nobody.'

This seemed to unnerve Charlotte. She looked around the room, fidgeting in her seat.

'I don't know what you're saying,' she said.

'Well, I think you do,' he said. He sipped his tea. 'I think everyone in this town knows. I'm the only one who hasn't been filled in on what goes on here.'

He then ate more of his toast; a statement to tell her that he had no more to say on the matter.

'Look, I need to go,' she said, getting up from her seat.

Philip grabbed her hand. It was much colder than his. Was this just because he'd had a very hot bath, or was she nervous?

'Please, Charlotte. I need to know what's going on here.'

She sat back down, and slumped in her chair as if to show defeat. He'd seen that kind of body language many times before when someone had had enough of lying and wanted to admit what they'd done. He was sure that Charlotte wasn't guilty in any way, but he was also sure that she knew more than she'd so far let on.

'Look,' she started. 'I'll tell you what I know. But don't let anyone know it came from me.'

Suddenly, Philip felt a little nervous. He didn't know what he was about to be told. What did she know about the creature that was roaming his house, and what else was there to know about Greysands? And why was it so important to lock your doors?

She looked him straight in the eye. This was something she'd rarely done on the few occasions they'd met so far. As lovely as Charlotte was, and even though she worked in the local pub, and no doubt had to deal with drunken customers now and then, she did come across to Philip as shy. But he was taken aback by the way she looked at him, partly because of her serious expression, but also because of her beauty, even when the smile had left her face.

Here it comes, he thought.

'Greysands is haunted.'

18

There it was. The answer to all his questions in one little sentence. There was no puzzle to work out at all. It was as simple as that. Greysands was haunted. She said it with such conviction that he almost felt bad for laughing.

'I'm serious.'

'Haunted?'

'Yes.'

He didn't want to offend her so he tried his hardest to stop smiling and to stop his shoulders from bouncing up and down. He did so by thinking of the creatures that had interrupted his sleep, stolen his chocolate cake and knocked him down the stairs. He didn't believe in ghosts, but something was going on.

'With the greatest of respect, Charlotte, ghosts don't exist.'

'That's what most people that move into this house think, but they feel very different by the time they pack up and move on.'

'Anyone who moves to Greysands, or just to this house?'

'Weird things go on in the town, but it's mainly centred around this house.'

'And has anyone ever got somebody to investigate?' he asked, thinking of David Ash from the James Herbert book he'd been reading in the pub. He was a paranormal investigator. It sounded to Philip that Greysands needed someone like him to come to the town and find out what was going on.

'I don't know; I don't think so. People just move on.'

Before Philip could ask any more questions, there was a

knock at the door. He stood to go and answer it but the dizziness came over him again.

Charlotte grabbed his hand. 'You sit down; I'll get it.'

As groggy as he was, he still felt a surge of electricity from Charlotte's hand touching his. Even though she'd just told him a story that he found laughable, he still felt something for her. The fact that she believed in ghosts just endeared her to him.

As Charlotte answered the door, Philip heard a voice he recognised.

'Oh, pardon me, Miss, but is this the home of Philip Lloyd?'

'It is, come in,' Charlotte said.

She led him through to the kitchen.

'Philip,' he said.

'Morning, Daniel,' Philip answered. 'I told you not to come.'

Daniel looked at him and briefly looked at Charlotte. Daniel was doing his best to hide his curious expression as he tried to weigh up why a young lady was answering Philip's door, and why he was in a dressing gown, but Philip could tell he was puzzled.

'Well, you sounded terrible on the phone so I thought I'd come and check on you.'

'Thank you,' Philip said. 'This is Charlotte. She works at the local pub.'

Daniel shook her hand. 'Daniel,' he said. 'Nice to meet you. I'm Philip's ...'

'Accountant,' Philip finished. 'He's my accountant.'

'Nice to meet you too,' Charlotte said.

Daniel took his coat off and put it on the back of the chair. He then sat his huge frame down at the kitchen table. Even when seated, he was still taller than Charlotte. He was a stocky, well-built black man who Philip always thought looked more like a bouncer than a literary agent. His very short hair surely should be showing some signs of grey for a man in his late fifties, but so far, not Daniel's.

'I'll leave you to it,' Charlotte said before going to the bottom of the stairs to put her coat on.

'OK, Charlotte. Thanks for calling. I'll probably be in the pub later,' Philip said.

'Bye now,' Daniel said.

Now with his back to the departing Charlotte, Daniel's eyebrows raised as if waiting for an explanation.

'What?' Philip asked. He wasn't in the mood for defending himself. After all it was Lesley who made him leave. And although he felt a little guilt, he hadn't actually done anything wrong; not as yet anyway.

'A young lady answering your door and you sat here in a dressing gown doesn't look good. Good job it's me that's called to see you and not Lesley.'

'There's nothing going on. I told you, I fell down the stairs. Charlotte just called to say hello, and when she saw what state I was in she ran me a bath.'

Daniel laughed. 'I know you're telling the truth, Philip. If there was something going on, she would be scantily dressed too. And you wouldn't look like crap. That's one hell of a bruise on your face. You should let me take you to hospital.'

'There's no need for that. I just need another nap, that's all.'

'Why didn't you want her to know I'm your agent?'

'In the few days I've been here, I've managed to avoid telling people who I really am.'

'What? Nobody knows who you are?'

'Not as yet. I've told the people my first name, but not my last.'

Daniel stood and walked over to the kettle to make himself a drink.

Philip knew he should've offered but he was still unstable on his feet, and his head continued to pound.

'Have you had any more contact from that woman?'

For a second Philip thought he was referring to Lesley, but he realised he meant Jade Romily.

'No. Nothing. Ah, but I've only just got a phone line and I haven't connected my laptop to the Internet yet.'

'Well you'll be pleased to know that nothing has been leaked to the press so far.'

'No?'

Daniel shook his head. 'But the bad news is, she sent the email and Lesley watched the video. I told her not to but she did anyway.'

This wasn't a surprise to Philip. He knew she wouldn't have been able to help herself, as torturous as it must've been for her to watch.

'Should I call her?'

Daniel turned back from putting a tea bag into the cup and looked him in the eye. 'I wouldn't; not yet.'

'Why?'

'To be honest, Philip, she asked me to help her choose a divorce lawyer.'

This was a surprise. Although Philip was enjoying his new life, he was still shocked to find out that Lesley was thinking about divorce so early. He thought she'd want to try again before taking such drastic measures.

'Well, I told her to think about it and I'd call her in a week. That was yesterday so there's still time for her to change her mind.'

'Maybe.'

There was a silence between them as Daniel finished making his tea.

'So,' Philip started, 'what about this new client of yours?'

'I've just changed the meeting for later in the day. I'll head back to Manchester after this drink.'

'It's a long way to come for a cup of tea.'

'Well you sounded terrible, and to be honest, I think I should be taking you to hospital, but over the last couple of decades, I've gotten to know how stubborn you can be.'

'I'm fine, honestly.'

'Well I'll make you a deal,' Daniel said.

'What's that?'

'I'll phone you tomorrow morning, and if your headache hasn't gone, I'll come back and take you to hospital.'

Philip begrudgingly accepted. 'Deal.'

'No lying to me though; I'll tell by your voice. And rest today. No writing. You won't be very good with a cloudy head anyway. Also, if you do go to the pub, stay on lemonade.'

'I will.'

Daniel took a gulp of his tea then looked around the kitchen from his seat. 'So, how are you settling in?'

'Great,' Philip said. 'It's an old-fashioned house in a town still stuck in the past, but that suits me just fine.'

'It's definitely old-fashioned; and a little creepy if you ask me.'

'Creepy?' Philip asked.

'Yes. It's like a house from a horror film. It's a pity you're not a horror writer; this place would be a brilliant inspiration for that genre.'

'Maybe I should give it a go at writing a horror story while I'm here.'

'You could,' Daniel said, with wide eyes. 'We could release it under a pseudonym.'

'I'll consider it.'

Philip thought that it wouldn't take much to come up with a story. A writer living on his own and being disturbed as he sleeps by strange creatures would be a good premise to start with.

'So how did you end up falling down the stairs?'

'I tripped and fell from half way down.'

'Had you been drinking?'

'I'd had one pint of bitter at the pub, and then I fell asleep on the sofa. It was ...' He struggled to decide on how much to tell Daniel. He considered him a friend, but they were only friends because he was his agent. If he retired from writing he probably wouldn't stay in contact with him, except for maybe a Christmas card.

No. Philip decided not to tell him. He also decided to keep Charlotte's story of ghosts to himself, for now at least.

'... it was on my way to bed in the middle of the night, I stumbled and fell.'

'Well you've had a nasty fall judging by that bruise. It's covering almost half of your face.'

Philip put his hand up to feel it. He winced as he made contact. He was aware of the pain but so far, it'd been overshadowed by the throbbing in his head. Now his headache was fading he was becoming more aware of how much his face hurt.

After asking Philip if he had any painkillers and Philip shaking his head, Daniel put his coat on and trampled through the snow to his car. He returned with some paracetamol and left him the box. After that, they said their goodbyes and Daniel went on his way.

Philip took two of the capsules with the last of his tea before lying down on the sofa once more. He thought that maybe he should phone Lesley once he woke up, but he wasn't sure. For now, he pushed any thoughts of divorce to the back of his mind, and drifted off to sleep, hoping that the phone wouldn't ring, nobody knocked on his door, and more importantly, no ghosts came to visit as he slept.

19

The clock said almost four-twenty as Philip opened his eyes. He could tell by the small amount of daylight coming through the window that it was afternoon, unlike the previous night when he'd been unsure just which three-twenty-five it was. After sitting up and stretching, he made himself a much-needed cup of tea. He then went and sat on the sill of the bay window, cup of tea in his hand, looking out over the ocean. Snow was falling again, but only lightly. He wondered how long the town of Greysands was going to stay under the blanket of white that was not only beautiful, but also felt as though it was protecting him from his old life.

Daniel might've made it through the snow to check on him, but most people wouldn't travel in conditions like this unless absolutely necessary. He was sure that Lesley wasn't going to turn up, for which he felt relieved. He knew he shouldn't feel that way. He knew he should be hoping to see her to try and convince her that their marriage *was* worth saving, but that wasn't how he felt. The truth was he didn't know how he felt.

He was a little worried about how much sleep he'd had since he fell, or was knocked, down the stairs. But now, after all these hours of sleep, he suddenly felt much better. His head wasn't hurting any more, and his face only hurt if he touched it or changed his expression, but other than that he felt fine.

He decided to do two things with the rest of the day. That evening he would speak to Charlotte and find out more about these ghost stories. But first, he thought a nice walk around the town would be a therapeutic way to spend what was left of the fading daylight, and he needed the fresh air. After finishing his tea, he went upstairs to brush his teeth and then put his winter coat and hat on, and left the house, being sure to lock his door, as the saying went.

The tide was in as Philip walked along the seafront, the waves gently crashing along the pebbled shore, making a swishing sound as they landed. He walked past the pub, then the cafe, then Karen's shop. After those three buildings the town seemed to be struggling. There was an empty shop that still had the old sign above it; Greysands Gifts. The next shop didn't have any signage, but Philip looked through the dirty window to see a large empty room with nothing but a pile of unopened letters sat on the floor. This seemed to be the pattern for the next six or seven shops until he came to the chip shop. It was closed, but the clean interior suggested it was still in business. He checked the list of hours on the window; it opened at five o'clock. It was nearly five by now, so Philip thought he'd come back later and try the local cuisine.

As he went past the shops, he saw the children's train track. This was a sad sight, much like the amusement park at the back of his property. He didn't think the train would have been used in winter anyway, but he could tell by the overgrown weeds making their way up through the miniature sleepers that it hadn't been used for many years. He wondered if the councillor had any plans to draw some funding from somewhere to repair these things and maybe advertise Greysands as a great place to come for a day out with the kids. But he didn't think so.

To Philip, Greysands was a beautiful place. It just needed

a little help to get back off the ground. He wondered if the councillor wanted to improve the town or whether he preferred things the way they were; everybody struggling to make ends meet and being under his control. Philip wanted to find out more, but he knew he should keep out of it.

He reached the bright lights of the arcade at the pier, although they weren't actually all that bright; many of them were flickering or out altogether. He walked through the doors and was greeted by the flashing lights of slot machines and arcade games. The room was filled with noises and music, but as he walked through the large room, he yet again felt the depression of the town as he realised that nobody was in there; no children, no adults, not even a member of staff sat in the booths waiting to give out change.

The coin pushers moved back and forth, the horse-racing game continued to send the little plastic horses down the track, even though no one was betting on them, and the air hockey machine flashed its lights, but the paddles lay still on the surface of the board.

Philip wasn't much of a gambler, so he kept walking through the room towards the back doors. When he reached them, he pushed them open and walked out onto the pier. The gaps in the wooden slats revealed the swishing ocean waves beneath. The deck was surrounded by a metal fence with flaking red paint.

He walked all the way to the end and stood overlooking the ocean. He pulled his coat collar up to shield his stinging face from the cold sea wind. As he turned to look back on the ghostly town, he saw the lighthouse standing on top of the hill. It looked only yards away from his house from this angle. The house looked even more creepy and haunted from this distance. He almost expected to see the curtains twitching or a ghostly figure move past one of the windows. After all, that's what would happen in a ghost story, wasn't it? But he saw no such movements.

He turned back to look over the ocean once more when suddenly he heard the arcade doors open. It was Charlotte. Her beautiful smile immediately made him forget how cold he was feeling. His heart seemed to skip a little every time he saw her. Yes, he was married. Yes, he was much older than her. But she seemed to keep turning up; twice at his house, and now on a walk through the town. He wasn't positive, but he was pretty sure she liked him.

'Long time, no see,' he said. 'A few hours at least.'

She walked over and stood next to him, leaning on the rail. 'Are you feeling any better?'

'Much better, thanks. I went back to sleep after Daniel left, but I'm feeling fine now.'

'That's good. Your bruise still looks painful.'

'It hurts in the cold wind, or when I smile, but apart from that its fine.'

They were silent for a couple of minutes. Philip wanted to ask more about the ghost story she'd started earlier that day, but he sensed that she was going to bring it up anyway.

'I'm sorry about before,' she said.

'What about?'

She wasn't smiling now. 'I shouldn't have said what I said. It was stupid.'

This confused Philip. 'Why was it stupid? Were you not telling the truth?'

She exhaled as she pondered what to say. Philip thought

perhaps she wasn't supposed to tell outsiders this secret. But he wasn't sure.

'What I said was true,' she said. 'Well, the locals all think it's true, but I don't know for sure. I shouldn't have said anything. I don't want you thinking that I want you to go, because I don't.'

'Why would I go?'

'Because everyone else who's ever moved into that house has gone within a few months.'

'I'm not planning on going anywhere.'

'Good,' Charlotte said.

She looked him in the eye. He thought it would be a good moment to kiss her, but he didn't. He didn't want to misread the situation, and he was still paying for the last time he'd come too close to another woman. He had no intentions of cheating on Lesley again, but he thought that maybe once he'd spoken to her, he could find out properly what she wanted, and then perhaps he could move on. Even though he wanted to kiss Charlotte, he didn't feel as though it was the right time.

He smiled at her; his face ached as he did so. Instead of kissing her, he decided to see if he could get to know her a little more.

'Come on,' he said. 'Let's go inside and get warm.'

The inside of the arcade wasn't much warmer than the outside, but at least they were away from the wind.

They sat on a bench next to the bumper car track after Philip had got them both a hot chocolate from the drinks machine.

He wanted to get to know more about her, and decided to steer the conversation around to her life, and not the creature or creatures that had been haunting him.

'So, tell me about you. I was going to ask you how long

you'd lived here, but I've been told that everyone who lives here was born here.'

Charlotte nodded. 'I was born here, yes.'

'And?'

'And what?'

Philip laughed a little. 'Tell me about yourself.'

'What would you like to know?'

He shook his head. 'Everything.'

'There's not much to tell. I was born in Greysands. I've lived here all my life. I was well-behaved at school, but didn't go to college.'

She paused for a moment as if contemplating how much to tell.

She then said, 'My mum died when I was eleven, and my dad fell ill when I was sixteen, so I had to quit my education and get a job.'

'Really? Could you not have stayed at school and asked for Carer's Allowance?'

'My dad was quite well off, so money wasn't the problem. Before he was ill, he worked the sea.'

'Worked the sea?'

'He was a fisherman.'

'Oh,' Philip said. That was a term he'd never heard before.

'Only, he didn't just have one boat like everyone else, he set up more boats and hired staff. He had twelve vessels at his most successful time. Normally fishermen work for other boats, save up, and then set up on their own. But my dad was a generous boss, and he gave paid holidays instead of making the staff stay as self-employed. Because of this, his staff stayed loyal to him and made a good living themselves, so had no need to leave.'

'Sounds like a clever man.'

'He was. But when I was sixteen, he fell ill with lung cancer. I left school to look after him and worked part-time in the evenings at the chippy.'

'Until you were old enough to work in the pub?' Philip asked.

'It wasn't my intention to end up working in the pub. I started in the chippy, then got a job in the cafe, and then I got a job in here at the arcade. I wanted to work part-time so I could be available for my dad, but I ended up with three part-time jobs. Once I was eighteen, I asked for a job in the pub, simply because my dad slept all evening, so it made sense to be at home through the day and working at night. I didn't really need to work at all because as I say, my dad was quite wealthy. But I didn't want him to see the money he'd worked so hard for disappear while I cared for him. I wanted to bring a wage in, even if it was just a small one.'

'I understand that,' Philip said. 'A lot of pressure for a girl of that age though. Did you not have any help from other family?'

'No. My grandparents had already died. My parents had me quite late you see.'

'I see. Is your father still with us?'

She shook her head. 'He fought a brave fight. He fought it for fifteen years before ...' She choked up a little and couldn't finish her sentence.

Philip put a hand on her arm.

'Anyway, he left me the house and what was left of his money, so I do OK. I don't consider myself wealthy, but I'm comfortable. And my wage from the pub is enough to live on, and there's no mortgage on the house, so I get by all right.'

'Can I ask how old you are?' Philip asked.

'Philip ... you're not supposed to ask a lady that,' she said, smiling.

'I know; but I can't quite place your age. You could be late twenties, but you act more mature than that, so I'd guess at early thirties,' he said, making sure he was well under what he actually thought. She was very pretty – beautiful, even – but he couldn't place her age.

'You're being silly. There's no way you think I'm in my twenties.'

'Well, I'm not too sure,' he said, throwing a smile at her.

'I'm thirty-nine, if you must know.'

He raised his eyebrows in surprise. 'Really?'

'Yes,' she said, trying hard not to blush. But Philip could tell by her coy demeanour that she was flattered.

'So, what about you?' she said. 'What brought you to Greysands?'

He thought for a moment. He didn't want to share too much, and he didn't want her to know about his recent behaviour.

'I needed a fresh start. My wife and I have separated, so rather than be around our friends, and things feeling awkward, I decided to move away. They are mostly her friends anyway.'

'Don't you have any of your own friends?'

'I have, but I don't see them very often. They're people I phone every now and then to catch up, but that's all.' He realised how pathetic that sounded. The truth was, he was so wrapped up in his writing career, that he'd lost touch with everyone. There are only so many times you can say no to invitations before the invitations finally stop.

He began to wonder if it was the right time to ask Charlotte about the events of the last few days. He certainly didn't want to talk about his marriage.

He took another sip of his hot chocolate before saying, 'Look, Charlotte. I've moved here to get away from a complicated situation. I love this town and the way I feel at the moment, I want to stay. How long for, I don't know. But I do want to stay.'

'I hope so,' she said.

'But I have a problem.'

She looked a little confused.

'Weird things are going on in my house, and if you can tell me what's going on, I might be able to deal with it better. Maybe if I understand a bit more, I can be ready for what happens next. And with the greatest of respect to you, I don't believe in ghosts.'

'But you've read *Haunted*. You said so.'

'Just because I like reading ghost stories doesn't mean I believe in them.'

'I suppose,' she said. 'I never used to believe in ghosts, but everyone who's lived at the park house has said that the place was haunted.'

'There has to be more to it. And you actually said that Greysands is haunted. What does that mean?'

'Well ... yes. Weird things happen in the town as well,' she said.

'Like what?'

'You'll see,' she said.

This was the most cryptic thing she'd said so far.

He waited.

Finally, she said, 'Things going missing from people's gardens. People finding doors open.'

'That's why people keep telling me to lock my doors?'

Once again, she looked as though she didn't want to talk about it. Her gaze shot around the room.

'Come on,' she said, jumping up off the bench. 'Let's have a go on something. How about air hockey?' She rummaged in her coat pocket and pulled out a pound coin before putting it into the slot. The table lit up as air began to blow through the little holes.

'I'd rather finish our discussion,' Philip said.

Charlotte grabbed one of the paddles and moved around the table. 'Come on, there's a time limit you know.'

The conversation was obviously over. The two of them spent the next hour or so playing several different machines throughout the arcade. They even had a go on the bumper cars. Despite being fifty-five, Philip felt very young in Charlotte's company, especially today. He didn't think anyone else could get him to have an hour of being silly and playing the arcade games. He almost forgot how old he was as they moved from machine to machine. Although he didn't get anything else from Charlotte about the goings-on of the town, he certainly enjoyed her company. And he hoped he could spend more time with her.

20

After saying goodbye to Charlotte as she headed off to work, Philip called at the chip shop and bought two portions of fish and chips. He was expecting them to come wrapped in newspaper as everything else in the town seemed to be based on habits and customs from yesteryear, but this wasn't the case. They came wrapped up in white paper and put into a plastic carrier bag with the shop's logo printed on the side.

Philip walked through the snow back towards his house; only he went past it and headed for the lighthouse. He had a quick look through the window from the road, but as it was dark by now, he couldn't see anything. Again, he was expecting to see movement, but he didn't. As the day moved on, he started to doubt what happened the previous night. Maybe it was a dream, he thought. Or maybe some form of night terror caused by his recent change of life. He didn't know. But the bruise on his face was real.

He really liked Charlotte. He also had a lot of respect for her; especially now he knew her story. Although he didn't know her very well, he still thought she was somebody he could trust and had no reason to think she would lie to him. But ghosts weren't real, so why would she think that the house and the town were haunted?

He pressed the intercom on the lighthouse and moments later Tom answered.

'Hello,' he said.

'Tom, it's Philip.'

'I'll be right down.'

Three or four minutes later, an out-of-breath Tom opened the door.

'Well, good evening, Philip.'

'Good evening to you, Tom. I've brought you some supper.'

'You'd better come in then.'

After climbing the seemingly endless stairs of the lighthouse, and Tom had made them a cup of tea, they both sat down to eat. Not with plates or cutlery. Chippy chips and fish, straight from the paper, just how Philip liked it. It reminded him of his life before he'd earned his fortune. Lesley wouldn't let him eat like this. It's not what wealthy people do, apparently.

'So, what have I done to deserve this then?' Tom asked.

'Nothing really,' Philip answered. 'Well, you bought me a pint of bitter, and you were kind enough to let me visit this magnificent building. And I remembered you saying that your wife used to bring you a chippy tea.'

'Well, that's very kind of you,' Tom said. 'So, how are you settling in?'

'I'm doing just great. I love the house and I love the town.'

'That bump to your head didn't put you off then?'

Philip hadn't forgotten about the previous night's events, but he had briefly forgotten about his bruised face.

'Err ... no. It's not put me off. I fell down the stairs, that's all.'

'Oh, I know what happened,' Tom said, putting another chip into his mouth.

This confused Philip. 'How?'

After he finished chewing, he took a swig of his tea. 'I saw Charlotte as she left your house this morning. She told me about the fall.'

'You can't keep secrets in Greysands, can you?'

'You'll be amazed at what secrets you can keep in Greysands,' Tom answered.

'Really?'

'So, what happened?'

The vague comment from Tom hinted at more goings-on. But as usual, the subject was changed as quickly as it started.

'I fell down the stairs.'

There was a silent moment as this statement was left unchallenged. Philip thought Tom would want to know more, but he just left it where it was.

Philip thought that now was as good a time to ask Tom about the events in his house. He wondered whether he should ask about ghosts, but considering the guarded way Charlotte had told him about the town being haunted, he thought he'd come at it from a different angle.

'So,' he said. 'Moving to this town hasn't been as uneventful as I thought it would.'

Tom looked up from his supper. 'How do you mean?'

'Well ... the strange things that happened.'

Tom didn't speak.

Philip was starting to think that Tom wasn't interested in continuing the conversation from their meeting in the pub. Most people would want to know straight away what the strange things were. But Tom seemed very calm and patient about the story.

'Do you not think it's strange?'

'In what way?'

'An intruder in my house.'

'You could've been dreaming,' Tom said.

'I was awake last night when I was knocked down the stairs.'

Tom took another sip of tea before saying, 'I thought you were hinting at ghosts, but ghosts don't push you down the stairs.'

'Did you think the house was haunted?'

'No,' he said. 'I've heard stories of strange things going on there, but I don't believe in ghosts.'

'Is it just the park house, or are there strange things going on elsewhere in the town?'

Tom scratched his head as if he was thinking of an answer. Eventually he said, 'Some people would say that weird things happen all over the town, but it's the park house that gets people talking the most, and the amusement park itself.'

'Really?'

Tom nodded.

'What happens at the amusement park?' Philip asked.

Tom stopped to think again. 'Noises mainly,' he said.

'What kind of noises?'

'Banging,' he said. 'Screaming.'

Philip's suddenly felt nervous. 'Screaming?'

'Yeah. I wouldn't worry.'

Philip laughed, although he didn't find anything about this conversation funny. '*I wouldn't worry*?' he said. 'I've been pushed down the stairs and people hear screaming, but you say not to worry. At what point should I start worrying?'

'It's mostly just rumours. Nobody has ever said they've seen anything concrete. It's all just drunk talk.'

Philip leaned over the table and looked Tom in the eye. 'Have you ever seen or heard anything coming from the house or the park?'

Tom let out a sigh before finishing his tea. 'You might say that.'

Philip's eyes opened almost as wide as his mouth as he waited for more.

Eventually Tom said, 'I've seen movements.'

'Movements where?'

'In the park, at night ...' he said. He seemed to stop halfway through a sentence.

Philip waited again for more.

'And through the windows of the house.'

Philip sat back in his chair. He was angry, but he wasn't quite sure who with. Tom and Charlotte seemed to be nice people, but if they were nice people, shouldn't they have warned him as soon as he moved in?

'What's going on in this town, Tom? You all seem to be keeping some sort of secret from me. People stop talking when I enter a room, people keep telling me to lock my doors, everyone seems to know something I don't. What is it?'

Tom looked a little flustered. 'Look. You now know as much as me. People have been talking about the park house being haunted for years and there possibly is some truth to it because you're the fourth tenant that place has had since Councillor Fisher's dad was alive. So, something is going on.'

'Hang on,' Philip said. 'You've told me about him before. Is that where he lived?'

'Yes. Didn't I say?'

'No, you didn't. So, I'm guessing that Councillor Fisher is my landlord?'

'Well, sort of.'

'How do you mean?'

'He still owns the amusement park, but he sold the house.'

'I see. Do you know who to?'

Tom shook his head. 'Just a private landlord I think.'

They sat in silence for a moment.

Philip felt something rub against his leg. When he looked, it was Daisy, Tom's whippet. He stroked her head as she sat next to him. He liked dogs, and had one as a child, but never as an adult. But he did like them and always went out of his way to pet them when he got the chance. But as much as he liked dogs, he had other things on his mind at that moment.

'So, what happens now, then?' Tom asked.

'In what way?'

'Are you going to move on?'

This question surprised Philip. 'Is that how easily people usually give up?'

'They normally last a few months; occasionally longer.'

'Well the way I look at it, ghosts don't exist so whatever it is can be dealt with.'

'That's the spirit,' Tom said. 'How are you going to deal with it?'

'By asking a local lighthouse-keeper to help me.'

Tom's eyes opened wide. 'Me?' he said. 'What can I do?'

'When do you finish?'

Tom checked his watch. 'Couple of hours.'

'Right then. After you've finished, come to the house. I've had plenty of sleep today so I'll stay awake all night if need be.'

'What are we going to do?'

'We're going to catch whatever it is that keeps *haunting* me.'

'Oh, I don't know about ...'

'Tom,' Philip said, 'I'm asking you nicely.'

Tom seemed to consider his options. Obviously, he could point-blank refuse, but Philip didn't think that was going to be the case. Moments later he begrudgingly said, 'OK.'

21

Back at home, Philip switched on his laptop, not with the idea of writing, but just to look over the last chapter he'd written the previous day. He only had a couple of hours to kill, and didn't feel as though he had enough time to really get into writing his next chapter while he waited for Tom to arrive, so he just read over his work and did a little editing.

When he'd finished, he turned off his computer and stared at the new object that resided on his desk. The phone that Charlotte had given him was now working, so he thought, what the hell, and decided he'd call home; his old home that was.

After a couple of rings, Lesley answered. 'Hello?'

'Lesley; it's me,' Philip said.

She didn't reply straight away but he heard her draw a deep breath.

'I wanted to phone you to see how you are,' he said. 'Is that OK?'

There was another silence as he heard Lesley breathe in and out. Finally, she said, 'I don't know what you want me to say.'

'I want to know if you're OK. I want to know what you're thinking, how you are feeling. I want to know if it's too late for us, or if there's a chance we can fix this.'

'Fix this?' Lesley said, raising her voice. 'Fix this? You have drunken sex with a stranger who tries to blackmail you and you think we can just move on and act like nothing happened.'

He had no answer for that.

'We had a brilliant life,' Lesley said. 'A brilliant marriage too and you threw it all away.'

'A brilliant marriage?' Philip asked.

'Yes,' Lesley snapped back.

'You thought our marriage was good?' Philip asked.

'Yes. Didn't you?'

'Well, if married life is two people living together without ever being in the same room unless they're in bed with their backs to each other, then yes, that's what we had.'

'Oh, so that's why you did it? You weren't happy with our life.'

'I was happy with our life,' said Philip, 'but we weren't a happy couple. I'm not talking about sex here, sex slowly disappearing isn't unusual, but when was the last time we held hands, or you kissed me hello or goodbye? When was the last time we sat and had a conversation?'

'We spoke all the time,' Lesley said.

'Only if it was about writing. If you'd read something and had notes to tell me then you'd sit and speak to me, but that's all.'

Another silence.

'So, what are you saying, Philip? You don't want to stay married anymore?'

'I'm not saying that. Look, I did a stupid thing. I fell for it and I'm angry with myself and embarrassed. But you have to accept that our marriage wasn't such a happy one; not the last four or five years anyway. I think we can fix it if you want to, but we have to fix everything. Things weren't right before my mistake. What I did has just brought it all to light.'

'You really think I can rebuild our marriage with you after seeing that video?'

So, Daniel was right; she'd watched it. He knew she would. He'd hoped she wouldn't, which is why he told her before Jade Romily sent the email. But he was wrong.

'Look, Lesley ...' he started.

'No, you look, Philip,' she snapped. 'There's no getting past this.'

She inhaled deeply and then said, 'I want a divorce,' before ending the call.

He stared at the phone, hearing nothing but the flat tone coming through the receiver.

Philip was confused. He felt as though his marriage was something he should fight for. But as the minutes passed, all he could think of was Charlotte, and how much he was falling in love with Greysands. He didn't know which way to turn.

He set the phone on its cradle and looked through the window waiting for Tom to arrive. Moments later, he did.

22

Tom walked in, carrying a carrier bag, with Daisy at his side. The snow was falling a little heavier by now, so Tom brushed his shoulders before removing his coat and handing it to Philip.

'I'm wondering if it might be better to take Daisy home first,' Philip said.

'No, she'll be fine. She can protect us; alert us to any danger.'

Philip looked down at the skinny frame of Tom's whippet. She was shivering, even though she was wearing a dog coat. Philip didn't think Daisy would be much use if anything was to happen, but nodded anyway before leading them through to the living room.

Tom seemed a little nervous to Philip as he looked around the room before finally sitting down on the sofa. Daisy climbed up and lay next to him. Philip didn't mind this; after all, it wasn't really his sofa.

'So,' Tom started, looking around the room once more. 'What do you want to do?'

'I think we should just sit here and wait for whoever or whatever to show its face,' Philip said.

Tom leaned forward and rummaged through the carrier bag that was now sitting on the floor. 'Well, it's a good job I brought this then,' he said, taking a full bottle of single malt whisky from the bag.

'I'm not sure that's such a good idea,' Philip said. 'I think we should keep a clear head if we're ...' he couldn't think what to call it. He certainly didn't want to refer to it as ghost-hunting. '... keeping a vigil,' he finished.

'Nonsense,' Tom said. 'A little tipple will keep us alert and give us the confidence we might need. Also, whisky is my drink. I couldn't drink more than five or six pints of beer, but whisky, whisky I can hold really well, so I'll still be alert.'

'Really?'

'Yes. It just agrees with me. I don't know why.'

'I'll get a couple of glasses,' Philip said, and went through the dark hallway to the kitchen.

After getting two small tumblers from the cupboard he turned and almost jumped out of his skin.

'Jesus!' he shouted at the small grey shape standing behind him on the floor. At first, he thought it was one of the creatures. Then he quickly realised it was Daisy. She'd followed him into the kitchen.

'What is it?' Tom shouted from the living room.

He didn't come running to investigate though. Perhaps he'd chosen the wrong person to help him, Philip thought.

'It was just Daisy. She made me jump.'

'Oh. She followed you in. She must like you,' Tom called.

Philip put the glasses down and took a cereal bowl from the cupboard and filled it with water. He set it down on the floor and Daisy had a couple of licks. Philip then turned off the kitchen light and walked back through to the living room, followed by his new companion.

'Thank you,' Tom said, taking the glasses from Philip and cracking open the seal on the bottle.

'I'm not really a spirit drinker. I'll only have a small glass,'

Philip said.

Tom poured them both three fingers, almost as if he hadn't heard Philip speak.

Philip sat in the armchair furthest away from the window. Tom was on the sofa facing the fire.

Philip took a sip of the single malt. He couldn't remember the last time he'd had whisky, but the smell that burnt his nostrils and the taste that numbed his throat reminded him that this was a drink he didn't cope well with. He'd much prefer a pint of bitter, but Tom brought whisky, so he had to be polite and have one glass at least.

'Why is it so dark in here?' Tom asked.

The only light came from the small reading lamp on top of the desk in front of the bay window, and the burning log fire.

'The two times I've been visited by this thing, well, the two times I'm aware of, were both at night when it was dark.'

'So, you're hoping something does turn up then?'

'I'd much rather they came back when someone else was here with me. For two reasons really; one, to help me catch it; and two, so I know I'm not going crazy.'

'Well let's see what happens.'

23

The clock on the wall had just turned to midnight and Philip was finding the single malt quite an enjoyable drink after the third glass. He wasn't feeling drunk but he was aware that he was under the influence. He certainly wouldn't try to drive his Mercedes the way he felt, but he still felt clear-headed enough to be ready should any visitors arrive.

Philip and Tom had spent the last couple of hours talking. Although the conversation was a little slow at first, as the evening went by, Philip began to find Tom more and more interesting. He spoke about his wife, his working life, and how he became the lighthouse keeper.

Philip spoke about his own life; his time in the police force, his marriage, and how it was coming to an end. He managed to keep his recent indiscretion to himself for now, and he told Tom he worked from home, but he didn't tell him about his writing career and how famous he was. He still hoped to keep that a secret for the time being.

'I'm wondering if we should sit quietly for a bit,' Philip said. 'Not that I'm not enjoying our conversation, but I'm wondering if we've more chance of it appearing if we're quiet.'

'You're probably right,' Tom said. 'One thing though; what are we going to do if it does appear?'

'That's a good point,' Philip said. 'Wait here.'

He got up and went through to the kitchen. He looked in the tall cupboard where the vacuum cleaner and other cleaning items were kept. He picked up a sweeping brush and a mop handle that was leaning against the back of the cupboard, detached from the mop head that lay on the floor.

He took them through to the living room and stood the brush up against the sofa where Tom was sitting. He then sat back in his chair, leaning the mop handle up against the wall as he did so.

'I'm not doing your housework,' Tom said.

Philip laughed. 'These will do as weapons.'

'Is a kitchen knife not better?'

'No. Not until we know what we're dealing with. We don't want to stab each other, or Daisy for that matter, by panicking at any movements that catch us off guard. Anyway, if the locals are right about ghosts then weapons won't be of use anyway.'

'True.'

They sat still, and they didn't speak. An hour passed by in the dark living room of the park house while they waited for something to happen.

Philip went upstairs and brought down a blanket for each of them. Tom stayed sitting upright but covered his lower half with it. He also covered Daisy's torso as she slept next to him, her head facing away.

'I tell you what,' Philip said. 'I'll turn the lamp off; the light from the fire should still be enough for us to see.'

'Err ... OK,' Tom said, sounding slightly wary.

The silence was deafening to Philip. He was used to being in a room with no noise. Being a writer, he had to work in silence. But there was something strange about being in a room with another person and not speaking to them.

As the time moved on and it headed further and further into

the early hours, he was starting to feel as though he might've wasted Tom's time.

A snorting sound came from Tom that made them both jump. Tom never opened his eyes as he stirred, but Philip did. He looked up at the clock on the wall. It was almost five in the morning. He must've been asleep for three or more hours. He hadn't had a disturbance this late before so he began to think that nothing was going to happen. He didn't realise he'd been asleep until Tom snored and woke him up. He didn't want to go to sleep but he couldn't fight off the effects of the whisky that Tom had forced upon him.

Philip gave in, closed his eyes, and went back to sleep.

24

A loud bang woke Philip up. He jumped; Tom did the same. Daisy gave a low whimpering cry as she jumped off the sofa. The light from the dying fire had faded and left the room in almost complete darkness.

'What ... what's happened?' Tom said.

'I think it's just the power going off.'

Although he couldn't see very well, he could hear Tom sigh as he shuffled in his seat.

'Bloody hell,' Tom said. 'Scared me to death.'

'Yeah,' Philip agreed. 'It went with a right bang that time.'

'Hang on,' Tom said. 'Why would it bang?'

'What d'you mean?'

'If it's another Greysands power cut it would just go off. Look out the window, Philip.'

Philip felt his way through the dark room to the window. As he pulled the curtain slightly open, he could see the snow falling over the town, brightly lit by the orange glow of the street lamp.

'Power's on. It must just be us. I'll get a candle.'

He rummaged through the drawer of his desk for a candle and the matches. Before he could strike the match, there was another sudden loud bang.

They both jumped and shouted out. Philip continued to strike the match and lit a candle with shaking hands.

He passed one to Tom. He then quickly lit another before

setting off to investigate the noise.

Tom got out of his chair and followed Philip through to the hallway; Daisy followed too, still whimpering.

Other than the tiny portion of orange glowing through the small glass square on the front door, the candles were the only light to help them see where they were going. Tom stood at the bottom of the stairs while Philip checked the kitchen. Just like the other times he'd heard bangs in the house, the doors and windows were locked. The two of them climbed the stairs slowly, one step at a time. Philip's legs felt weak, accompanied by a whisky headache and a dry mouth. He felt more scared now that Tom was with him. He thought it was because he might've imagined it before; he'd even considered the whole thing to be the sign of a breakdown, but two people can't have the same hallucination. Whatever was going on, it was real.

As they reached the top of the stairs, Philip decided to check the rooms on his own.

He put his hand on Tom's back and moved him a few feet away from the stairs before saying, 'You stay here. But be ready.'

Philip realised that they'd left their weapons downstairs, albeit just a mop handle and a sweeping brush, but still, they would've helped. He was so focused on the candles and the sudden, but ever more familiar, bang that he'd forgotten all about them.

He checked each of the bedrooms, and then the bathroom; as before, the house was empty.

They walked back down the stairs and went into the kitchen. Philip couldn't make the cup of tea he was craving, but he poured them both a glass of water and then started to wonder how to get the power back on.

'That's your problem,' Tom said.

'What?' he asked. He saw Tom heading over to the fridge.

'You've left the fridge door open. It'll have been working overtime and blown the fuse.'

Philip agreed with him as he closed the fridge door, but he didn't remember going into the fridge that night. And he was sure he'd have noticed the door open when he came into the room for the glasses when they started on the whisky.

'I've not been in there tonight,' he said.

'Well it's an old fridge. Maybe the seal is on the way out,' Tom said.

'Maybe. Where d'you think the circuit breaker is?' Philip asked.

'No idea,' Tom answered. 'In an old house like this it could be anywhere. Is there a basement?'

'Not that I'm aware of.'

They wandered around the downstairs rooms of the house looking for the box.

Philip looked around the kitchen and looked in all of the cupboards. He looked through the kitchen window. He couldn't remember seeing a shed or any kind of outbuilding, but he thought perhaps the circuit breaker was in a metal box fastened to the wall. He was pretty sure he'd seen boxes like that before on old houses, but couldn't remember when or where. He couldn't see much outside anyway because of how dark it was, but this didn't stop him from turning the key that was already in the lock of the back door.

'Philip,' Tom shouted.

Before Philip opened the door, he locked it again.

He walked back through to the hallway and was surprised

to see Tom standing at a wide-open door, leading to an area underneath the staircase.

'What the ...'

25

There was no handle on the door. It just looked like a wooden panel painted cream to match the surrounding wall. But he now could see that it *was* a door. Not just a door, but a door that would not only lead them – hopefully – to an electrical box, but also could shine a light upon the strange goings-on in the house. Maybe whatever it was was living down there.

Philip's pulse quickened. He found the discovery of a door very exciting, but also terrifying. He stood in silence as he looked into the deep, dark basement. The light from his and Tom's candles revealed the first couple of wooden steps, but nothing more. It also revealed the possible reason for the slamming door sound they'd heard that night; Philip had heard it a couple of times since moving into the house. He had to know if this was the sound he'd heard.

He took the panel door from Tom's grasp and gently swung it shut.

The bang was definitely the sound they'd heard. Was it a breeze that occasionally blew it open and shut? After all, the first time he heard it was when he closed the front door after his shopping trip. It could've been the backdraft of the front door closing. But it could also have been something else. Or even someone else. Could there be someone living in the basement? Surely not.

He pushed the door inwards which released it, swinging

towards him again. The push-to-open catch seemed to Philip to be the most modern invention in the whole house. He felt a little stupid for not realising there was a door under the stairs, and a basement. But now it was time to take his investigation a little further.

'After you,' Tom said.

Philip's heart was beating faster than ever. He wished that Daisy was a German shepherd or a Rottweiler, but unfortunately Tom's choice of a whippet for a companion was staying a good few feet behind them and certainly didn't want to lead the way.

The creaking of the first step made him jump a little. Not so much the noise, but how much it moved. He thought it was about to give way under him. It didn't so he continued to the next step.

The candlelight lit the narrow staircase as he took each step down into the basement. The smell reminded him of his shed at home, his real home. It had leaked and the damp had ruined most things that were in there. The basement had the same musty smell.

He still couldn't see to the bottom of the stairs. He was halfway down when he stopped to look behind him. Tom was still at the top holding the door in one hand and his candle in the other.

'Tom,' Philip whispered. He didn't know why he was whispering, but it felt like the right thing to do.

'What?' Tom whispered back.

'Are you coming?'

'I'd rather not,' he said.

'Tom,' Philip said.

Tom rolled his eyes before pushing the door wide open and making his way down the steps.

'Stay,' he said firmly to Daisy.

Philip couldn't see her from his angle, but presumed she did as she was told to.

They continued their descent, each step sending them a degree colder until it almost felt as though they were outside.

Just as they reached the bottom, the door slammed shut, making them both jump.

Tom dropped his candle; he then began to climb the stairs.

'Where are you going?'

'Someone's locked us in,' Tom said, flustered.

'Tom, wait. It's just swung shut; that's all.'

Tom stopped. 'Are you sure?'

'Quite sure,' Philip said. 'Come on. Let's get the power back on.' He almost added *and see what's down here,* but he didn't. He didn't want to scare Tom and he didn't want to unnerve himself any more than he already was by saying a line that sounds like it's come straight from a horror movie.

Philip moved the candle slowly from side to side to look at the basement. The low ceiling was covered by bare wooden beams that supported the floor above. The walls were red brick. He quickly realised that the basement wasn't one big room, but all separate rooms, divided by the red brick walls almost like a maze. Several boxes sat on the floor up against the walls. He saw an ancient lamp with its old-fashioned shade tilted to one side, the fringe covered by dust and cobwebs. There was a rusted lawnmower. A scrappy looking wooden door lay on its side against the wall, along with many other items from the past.

Philip began to walk around the basement. He had a choice

of turning left or right at the bottom of the stairs, but he chose to go left. The basement was freezing cold, so much so that the heat from the candle, as he shielded it to stop it from blowing out, was a welcome relief. He looked up and down at all the clutter, also checking the walls for any signs of the electrical box.

He could feel Tom walking closely behind him; both their footsteps shuffled on the dusty floor as they walked. Tom was breathing loudly. He was either very unfit, or very scared; Philip knew he climbed the lighthouse steps every day, so it must've been fear, he thought. The brick corridor came to an opening in the basement that led to another room. He walked in and held the candle high to light it.

'Shit!' he shouted, as his heart almost leapt from his chest. He quickly realised that the creepy face he saw looking back at him from a chair in the corner of the room was a clown, a toy clown, almost like a puppet. It was draped over the chair but its face was looking directly at them. It was only about two feet in length, but had the most horrific expression on its face. It wasn't quite as evil looking as Pennywise from Stephen King's *It*, but it wasn't far behind.

He had to go over to it and pick it up, to make sure it wasn't real, if he was honest. A clown doll coming to life and haunting him would've explained the mysterious events since moving into the house. He was still set on not believing in ghosts, but he needed to check it wasn't real.

He passed it to Tom who was still breathing heavily. He shook his head, refusing to touch the creepy-looking toy. Philip thought about sending him upstairs to relight his candle, but they'd come this far so they might as well carry on with their mission.

There were other toys scattered around the room, including a rocking horse in the opposite corner to the clown. But there was still no electrical box.

Tom's breathing was becoming more and more laboured. Philip was starting to think he shouldn't be putting the old fellow through this. He hadn't made many friends as of yet so it was either Tom or Charlotte. Although he wanted to get the electricity back on, he also desperately wanted to find an answer to the mystery of his late-night visitors. But he thought, for now at least, he should just get the power back on and let Tom go home.

The next room along, which was behind the staircase, was the most cluttered. There were boxes piled higher than the doorway; in fact, Philip realised, that this room was filled with boxes and nothing else. He opened the lid on one and found it was filled with cardboard cups. He didn't understand why anyone would have something like that in their basement. He opened another box, as he pulled on the cardboard flaps, he saw it was filled with plastic cutlery.

'Philip,' Tom said. Tom was standing behind him in the doorway.

As Philip turned, he saw him pointing at the wall just in the inside of the room.

The electrical box was on the wall just above the floor. Considering how old the house and everything inside it was, the circuit breaker looked very new.

Philip held the candle up to it and saw that of the six fuses that were there, five of them had a little green window and one had a little red window. He flicked the red one open and then pushed the bigger switch on the side, which brought the power back on.

They were still in the dark but Philip could hear the fridge above them come back to life.

'Done,' Philip said.

'Right,' Tom started. 'Can we get out of here now?'

Philip wanted to keep looking. He wanted to look through the basement for his own curiosity's sake, but he also wanted an answer to the disturbances. However, Tom's heavy breathing made him think it was time to let him go home. He also wanted to go upstairs and check the fridge door was staying shut in case it tripped the switch again. So, they called it a night and made their way out of the basement.

Philip thanked Tom for his help. Even though it was almost morning, Philip definitely needed to sleep. He dragged one of the armchairs through to the hallway and pushed it up against the door to the basement. Although he knew he wasn't done with the basement yet, he wanted to sleep and thought that blocking the doorway was the best way of dealing with it, for now at least.

He climbed the stairs and went to bed and was asleep within minutes of his head hitting the pillow. He knew he'd be back in the basement when he woke up, but for now, it had to wait.

26

The next morning, albeit late morning, Philip came downstairs after showering to find Daniel at his desk, looking out of the window while drinking a cup of tea. Of all the strange things going on since he moved to Greysands, this seemed the strangest. He momentarily thought that Daniel had died and this was his ghost visiting him. He remembered an early episode of *The X-Files*, when Dana Sculley's father died and she'd seen an apparition of him in the chair in her living room moments before the phone rang with the news of his death. Philip briefly wondered if this was happening to him.

Daniel turned around in the chair and greeted him as he walked into the room. 'Morning, sleepy head,' he said.

'What ... how ... how did you get in?' Philip asked.

'Well it's nice to see you too,' he said, smiling. 'You left the door unlocked. I presumed you'd had a late-night session so rather than come and wake you I made a pot of tea.'

Philip laughed to himself at the fact that in a town where everyone kept telling him 'lock your doors,' he'd forgotten and left it unlocked.

He looked on his desk and saw the teapot – which he didn't know he had – and a cup waiting for him, sat neatly on a tea tray.

'Still two sugars?' Daniel asked as he poured the tea.

'Yes, two please.'

Philip walked around and sat on the sofa.

Daniel handed him the drink that he was more than ready for. The headache from his fall had gone, but he felt a dull ache behind his eyes, which he suspected was more connected to whisky and the late night rather than his stumble down the staircase.

He couldn't believe that he'd left the door unlocked. He had a bit of an OCD for checking doors were locked, especially in his creepy new house. With everything going on the night before, he must've forgotten.

'What brings you here, Daniel?'

'You didn't look well when I last saw you. I said I'd phone you, but I thought I'd better come and see that you're OK. That bruise on your face isn't quite as bad though,' he said, leaning forward to get a better look at him.

Philip put his hand to his face. 'Still hurts.'

'Why are you up so late? Was it a late-night session?'

'Sort of, but not writing.'

'What does that mean?'

He wondered how much to share with Daniel. He was still very tired and he didn't like the idea of discussing ghosts when he felt this way.

'Err ... the power went off so I spent a long time getting it back on. And Tom, the local lighthouse keeper, called around with a bottle of whisky.'

'Ah, so that's why you're up so late.'

Philip nodded.

'How's your new novel coming along?'

'Very well,' Philip said. 'I think I'll be finishing the first draft within the next few weeks.'

'That's quick. I thought you'd be another month or so. When

will it be ready for me? I know Lesley normally proofreads for you.'

'Normally. I think I'll be OK without her, but you might get a few more mistakes than usual. I'll send it to you when I've completed my third edit; if I'm happy with it of course.'

Philip's process of preparing a novel was always, first draft, then edit while making changes to the story, then the third draft checking continuity, and then one final draft of checking everything, including and especially spelling mistakes.

'Did you think about what we talked about yesterday, about writing a horror story under a pseudonym?'

'I thought you were joking,' Philip said.

'Not at all,' Daniel said, standing up and walking around the room. 'Look at this place; if it doesn't inspire a writer to write a ghost story, I don't know what will.'

'Perhaps I'll give it a go.'

'Perhaps? Look around you; the log fire, the old carpets, the dark rooms, the creaking floors. It's a horror writer's dream come true.'

Philip smiled. 'I think you might be right.'

They spent the next hour discussing ideas, which was something they'd done many times over the years. Philip enjoyed this part of their relationship. Although Daniel wasn't a novelist himself, he knew the business inside out and when the two of them bounced ideas off each other, sometimes the process would create pure gold while filtering out the useless sediment along the way. Philip occasionally tried to stick to his guns when he felt strongly about an idea, but Daniel would always be proven right, even if Philip wouldn't admit this to him.

'Well,' Daniel said, looking at the time on his phone. 'I'd

better head back.'

'OK. Thanks for coming. Although you didn't have to, I'm perfectly fine. It's a long drive from Manchester.'

'It's no problem. You still look a little peaky. I'd get some more rest if I was you.'

'I will.'

As Philip held the door open for him, letting the cold winter breeze into the hallway, he thought he'd ask about Lesley. Even though he would rather just concentrate on his writing, and the ghostly adventure he'd found himself in since moving to Greysands.

'I briefly spoke to Lesley yesterday. Have you heard from her?'

'Not since we last spoke, no.'

'So, there's nothing new to tell me?'

'No,' Daniel said, walking away. He then turned back and said, 'Look, Philip, I don't really like being in the middle between you and Lesley. I still have to talk to her occasionally because of her handling your press, but I don't want to be involved with your divorce, or your ... misdemeanour.'

'I know,' Philip said.

'If she asks me to pass a message on, I'm more likely to tell her to speak to you directly rather than acting as a go-between. Don't get me wrong, I've known you a long time and our relationship is more than just a working one, or at least I hope it is. But I like you both and I'd like it to stay that way. I don't want to dread talking to either of you.'

Philip nodded. 'I understand.'

They said their goodbyes and Daniel walked down the path to his car.

Philip waved a hand before closing the door and heading

to his desk.

27

Philip could just about see the door to the basement from his writing desk, if he leaned back far enough. The door to the living room was always open. He wondered if he did that subconsciously so he could listen for any bangs in the house, or whether he'd just kept the door open ever since moving in anyway. The first loud bang he heard was just as he returned from his shopping trip to Karen's and that was only a couple of hours after his arrival, so perhaps he'd been listening for noises ever since he first sat down to write in his new home.

His writing wasn't going well today. He'd only written a few lines and they weren't very good. He always struggled to concentrate if there was something else going on in his life. All he could think about was the basement, and what else could be down there other than the unused plastic cutlery and that rocking horse and of course, the creepy clown.

He felt as though the clown needed a name. Pennywise would be too obvious, and it was far too creepy to be called anything fun like Bobo or even Krusty. He thought of all the old creepy clowns like Weary Willie, but none seemed to fit.

Then he remembered watching *American Horror Story*. The clown he saw in that was about as creepy and disgusting as you could get. The only problem was, he couldn't remember his name. He seemed to remember it being a fun-sounding clown name, which he thought made the character even better as a horror villain. He knew the name was in his brain somewhere, but he couldn't find it. He still hadn't connected his laptop to the Internet and didn't want to just yet. But he really did want to know that clowns name.

John Carroll Lynch.

The actor's name popped into his head, so at least he was halfway there. But he knew if he was going to think of it, he had to let it go. These things had a habit of jumping into your head when you'd least expect it, like when you're drifting off to sleep, or having a shower, or eating a sandwich at the dining table. So, for now, he tried to forget it.

He didn't use the Internet that much. Lesley ran his social media pages – hopefully, he thought, she was still doing so in a professional manner so as to not hurt the franchise that is Philip Lloyd – so he didn't feel the need for access to the information superhighway very often. Just occasionally to look up geographical queries as they came up during his writing. He didn't want to have to answer emails at the moment, so he was determined not to connect the laptop to the Wi-Fi.

Philip got up from his seat and walked over to the basement door, then looked back at the clock on the wall through the living room door. It was almost eleven o'clock in the morning. Still early considering how late he went to bed.

Philip made his decision. He was going to investigate now. Even though he was on his own, he still wanted to go into the basement.

He dragged the armchair away from the door. His heart began to beat a little faster as he prepared to open it. Before he did, he went into the living room to get the mop handle that was still leaning against the sofa. They forgot to take it into the basement the night before, but he definitely wanted a weapon of some sort if he was going down there alone.

As he returned to the basement door, he was just about to push it open when a bang made him jump.

At first, he thought it was one of the noises he'd heard before, but then realised it was a knock at his front door.

He rested the mop handle against the armchair that was still sat blocking the hallway and went to answer it.

Charlotte was standing there in the snow; which Philip was more than happy about. But he was confused to see Daisy, shivering next to her.

'Sorry to bother you, Philip. Can I come in for a second?'

He stood aside as Charlotte walked into the house, Daisy on a lead in one hand and a bulging supermarket hessian bag-for-life in the other.

'What's happened?' Philip asked. 'Is Tom OK?'

'No,' Charlotte said. 'He isn't.'

Philip's stomach sank.

'I live two doors away from him. I noticed his door open when I was walking by. I went inside and found him unconscious on the floor in the hallway, with Daisy lying next to him.'

'Oh no,' Philip said. He felt worried for Tom, but he also felt guilt for possibly causing unnecessary stress on someone who was obviously a very unhealthy man, even though he climbed the lighthouse steps every day.

'Luckily, he was well wrapped up in his coat and hat, but he leaves the lighthouse about nine, so he must've been lying there for about ten hours at least.'

'No. He didn't leave here until after five-thirty,' Philip said.

'How come?' Charlotte asked, looking confused.

'I'll explain later. Where is he now?'

'On his way to hospital. I was hoping you could look after Daisy for me, you know, with you working from home.'

'Sure,' he said. 'But can I come and see him too?'

'Yes,' Charlotte said. 'Get Daisy settled first.' She handed him the bag. 'I grabbed a couple of bowls and some tins of food and a blanket she sleeps on. Give me your phone number and I'll ring you when I know how he is.'

Philip ran to his desk and tore a piece of paper off his notepad. He took the telephone details from the desk drawer and wrote down his number, and walked back to the hallway and handed it to Charlotte. She in turn handed him the dog lead with Daisy still attached.

'Thank you for this, Philip. I'll phone you shortly.'

With that, she was gone.

Philip stood in the hallway with Daisy's lead in his hand. The dog looked up at him and gave a whimper, almost as if to say how she felt on the matter.

Philip looked down at her and said, 'I know.'

28

Philip desperately wanted to see Tom. He wanted to know if he was OK, but he also wanted to know if he blamed him for his heart attack, assuming that's what he'd had. Considering how he put away so much whisky the night before and listening to his heavy breathing, it could only be a heart attack, couldn't it? You'd have thought that climbing up and down the lighthouse steps would've been enough to keep Tom fit. But living on his own since his wife died could've been the cause. Philip was starting to understand how difficult it was to put any effort in to making a decent square meal when there was nobody to share it with. It was all too easy to just make a bacon sandwich or stick a ready-meal in the microwave rather than cooking anything that took any length of time. Perhaps this was a habit Tom had fallen into.

Philip emptied the bag that Charlotte had given him. There were three small tins of dog food, two bowls and a blanket covered in fine, grey and white dog hairs. He filled one of the bowls with water and placed it on the floor. After doing so he noticed the cereal bowl was still on the floor from the previous evening. Daisy chose her own bowl to drink from.

Philip then opened one of the small tins, got a spoon from the drawer and emptied the food into a bowl. He put it onto the floor and gently stroked Daisy's bony back as she ate.

'Well, Daisy. I'm not a religious person, but I hope to God that Tom's OK.'

Daisy didn't answer; not that he was expecting her to, but he still felt the need to say how he felt out loud.

He made a cup of tea as Daisy finished eating and wondered what to do next. Should he wait by the phone for it to ring? Should he get back to writing? Or should he take his mop handle and head into the basement in search of answers?

Philip opened the back door of the house for the first time since moving in. Daisy had a wander around the snow, sniffing at all four corners of the small garden that was still covered in deep, white snow. Philip looked over at the amusement park. He couldn't see as much of it as he could from the spare bedroom window, but he could see the tops of some of the rides and the shed's snow-covered roof.

Daisy crouched to relieve herself and then came trotting back into the house.

Philip was thankful when she came back inside quickly so he could close and lock the door, keeping at least some of the warmth from escaping.

He really wanted to go down into the basement, but the more he thought about it, the more he thought he shouldn't. He presumed Charlotte would be heading to the hospital in Blackpool, which was only twenty minutes or so from Greysands, maybe slightly longer because of the snow. But either way, there was a good chance she'd be phoning within the next half hour to let him know how Tom was doing.

He took Daisy's blanket through to the living room and laid it across one side of the sofa.

'Come on,' he said, tapping the blanket.

She jumped up and circled the area twice before lying down and making herself comfortable.

Philip thought that there was nothing he could do now until the phone rang, so he sat and watched the waves crashing back and forth through the window. The tide was high again and the higher the tide, the more beautiful the scenery. When it was out it was a long way out. So much so that he could hardly see the sea. When the tide was in, it not only gave the scenery more of a soothing, tranquil effect, but it also completed the perfect picture for him. The lighthouse, the crisp white snow, the pebbled beach and the waves making their way ever closer to the shore; he was falling more and more for Greysands. But if he was the cause of Tom's death, could he stay? Was running away and starting again going to become a habit for him? He hoped with all his heart that Tom would be OK. The wait was going to be agonising.

The phone rang. He'd fallen asleep again. He was beginning to make a habit of falling asleep in the daytime. He'd sat on the sofa next to Daisy and he must've drifted off.

He jumped up and answered the phone. 'Hello?'

He wasn't greeted by a voice. He wasn't greeted by any usual sentence that would normally come through the earpiece when answering the phone. He was greeted by a sniffing sound and then silence. In that moment, he knew. He knew that Charlotte was ringing him to say that Tom had died. She was obviously crying and couldn't get her words out, but Philip knew it was her, and knew why she was ringing.

'Charlotte?' he asked.

Another sniff, followed by a sobbing noise.

'Charlotte, I know it's you. Just take a breath and relax.'

He heard a deep but shaky breath whistle down the

phone line.

'He's gone, hasn't he?' Philip asked.

'Yes,' she said before crying hard into the phone. The word was hardly recognisable, but it answered his question.

'Do you want me to come and get you?'

More sobbing came, and finally she said, 'No. I'm with Karen.' The emotion then took a hold of her and she couldn't speak again.

'Hi, Philip,' Karen's voice.

'Karen, I'm so sorry. Tom was a lovely man. I don't know what to say.'

'It's OK, Philip. Look, I need to go because Charlotte needs me. We'll be back soon and we'll talk to you then.'

'OK.'

She hung up the phone.

He wanted to ask what Tom had died of, but that would've been selfish. It was true that if it turned out to be a brain haemorrhage, or a burst ulcer, then Philip would feel a little better knowing he hadn't assisted in the man's demise. But at that moment, all that mattered was how Charlotte was, and Karen and anyone else who'd known Tom longer than a few days. Philip had no right to put himself high on the list of people who were going to be affected by this, but he couldn't help but feel responsible. He was quite prepared to live with the guilt until a more appropriate time when he could ask more questions about what had happened.

For now, it was just him and Daisy in his new home. He began to wonder if the park house was about to become Daisy's new home too.

29

After pacing around the house for a couple of hours, and taking Daisy for a walk along the seafront – hoping to bump into someone who could tell him more about Tom, but unfortunately not seeing anyone – Philip decided it was time to venture into the basement.

He moved the armchair that he'd used to block the door, grabbed his mop handle and then opened the panel. He leaned inside and flicked the light switch on. A dangling twenty-watt bulb on the ceiling at the bottom of the creaky wooden steps partially lit the area.

He turned to Daisy and held his hand out. 'Stay,' he said in the same firm manner that Tom had used the night before.

Daisy sat still next to the opening.

Philip then began his journey down into the dark and dusty room, mop handle in hand at the ready. His pulse was racing as much as it had been the night before, only this time he felt even more nervous because he didn't have anyone helping him.

As he slowly reached the bottom, he looked left and then right at the two separate entrances to the red-bricked maze. The light only lit a small area. He looked around for more switches, but he couldn't see any. Then he noticed a light to his left, through one of the doorways. It was just as dim as the bulb at the bottom of the stairs but it was bright enough for him not to bother going back upstairs for a candle. The switch at the top must bring all the lights on in the basement, he thought.

He turned left as he had the night before. He walked into the first room and saw the creepy clown staring back at him. It didn't make him jump this time but the name of the clown did jump into his head the moment he set eyes on the hideous toy.

'Twisty,' he muttered to himself. That was the name of the clown from *American Horror Story*. And now that was the name of this clown too.

He picked up Twisty and threw him onto the bottom steps of the staircase, intending to take it up with him. It would make him feel a little better if it wasn't lurking below him in the basement. For some reason he thought it would make the basement less creepy if the clown wasn't down there. He knew his logic might be considered strange, but that was what he was going to do. Hopefully Daisy will chew it to pieces, he thought.

Philip continued into the next room where the electrical box was, plus the cardboard boxes he'd found, full of plastic cutlery. He looked around the room but there was nothing untoward in there. He couldn't see into the corners of the room because of the number of boxes, but from what he saw of the room it was clear to move on.

He headed back through the doorway and continued with his tour of the basement. He felt more and more cold the further he went. As he turned a corner, he noticed more doorways with dim lighting inside, just like the other two rooms.

The first room was almost empty, apart from a few tins of paint in the corner and a few rollers and trays; but as he reached the second room, his lungs sucked in a sudden gasp of air and he stood completely still. His stomach turned and he felt the sudden urge to urinate.

The room wasn't like the other rooms. This room was a

corridor; a very long corridor. Every twenty feet or so there was another light bulb hanging from the ceiling, but nothing else. It was just a long, straight, brick alleyway that headed off into the darkness.

He'd never been as scared as he was right now, not even when he was a police officer. He'd been trying to convince himself that he'd been imagining the bangs in the house, but then Tom backed up what he'd heard and now Philip stumbled on a corridor that didn't look like it belonged here or in any other basement he'd ever been in. Why was it there, and more importantly, where did it lead to?

He was colder now than ever, but he'd started sweating. His palms were wet and he could feel a drip working its way down the right side of his face. He felt like he was in a horror movie. The events that brought him to where he was shot through his mind; from the time when his life was perfect, or what he'd thought was perfect, to the indiscretion with Jade Romily, to moving to Greysands and meeting all the characters in the town, and even to the previous night where he'd possibly helped towards Tom's death.

Now he was standing at the entrance to God knows where. Was there a creature living down here? Should he phone the police? Should he go and trade his mop handle for a large kitchen knife?

He didn't know what to do.

And then he made his decision. He took a step forward as he began to venture into the dark and dusty corridor. Although he'd made the decision quickly, he was moving anything but.

The fact that he couldn't see the end of the corridor unnerved Philip. From where he was, it looked endless. After walking slowly and covering about ten feet, he stopped. It had suddenly occurred to him where he was and where he was heading.

People kept referring to his house as the park house. He gathered his bearings, the position of the staircase and how many turns it took him to get where he was. He realised that this tunnel was heading towards the amusement park. This was an underground connection between the park and the house. Although it'd been referred to as the park house, Philip had just thought it was called that because it was next to the amusement park. He didn't think that the two entities might've actually been connected, certainly not through an underground tunnel. That was why there were boxes of cutlery and cups in the basement. They were supplies for the park, possibly a cafe or food stall that was once there.

He couldn't decide if this made his fear depreciate or exacerbate. The amusement park was eerie and felt a little sinister. He didn't really know why. Perhaps it was the fact that no one really knew what went on in a fairground. To the people that lived and worked there it wasn't a job, it was a way of life; a life that they were embedded into whether they liked it or not. The generations of carnival folk that resided in these places lived their own lives by their own rules. Whether it was a travelling fairground or a stationary one, they had their own regulations. Minimum wage, statutory sick pay and holiday entitlements meant nothing in the world of the amusement park families. This was your life; like it or not, you got on with it.

Philip shuffled along the dusty gravel of the corridor floor, mop handle held out in front of him, almost like a Jedi with a light sabre. He'd never been so scared. He liked to think of himself as a strong character, someone who never shied away from anything, not when he was a police officer and not as an author. The two lives he'd led so far were very different. But in the early stages of his writing career, he'd have chosen to go into an inner-city riot with just his poly baton rather than stand in front of a room of prolific readers, reading a chapter from one of his books. It unnerved him, but he never refused to do an event, even though he suffered with terrible stage fright.

As he continued along the corridor, his heart leapt around his chest cavity, but he still walked on. He didn't want to phone the police with stories of bogie men waking him up at night. He wanted to know what he was dealing with, and hopefully deal with it on his own.

The endless corridor continued.

He looked behind him at the distance he'd covered – it was a good thirty feet. He felt even more vulnerable because he couldn't see to either end. All he could see was the dark corridor with the occasional low wattage light bulb lighting up a small area of the dusty tunnel.

Eventually, the end came into view, with the red brick wall giving the appearance of a dead end. As he got closer, Philip realised that it curved around to the left at a ninety-degree angle. As he continued around the corner, he was greeted by sudden blackness. There were no more bulbs hanging from the ceiling. It was pitch black.

The damp, musty smell was almost overpowering, but that was the least of his worries. He wanted to know what was down there.

He considered going back to get a candle, but he'd come so far, it just didn't feel right to turn back now. He walked slowly on, hoping his eyes would adjust to the blackness, which they did a little. But the further he walked, the further into darkness he fell. Looking behind, he saw the light from the last hanging light bulb disappear as he moved further and further away from it.

As he turned back to face the dark side of the tunnel, he realised he was now blind. He couldn't see, but continued to shuffle along in short steps, one hand holding out the mop handle, the other waving side to side trying to feel for the walls.

He eventually noticed light up ahead. The tunnel was still cold, but not like the temperature outside; more like inside of a garage or shed. As he got closer and closer to the light, his eyes tried to make sense of the shapes in the shadows up ahead; black shapes on the ground near the light. They looked black bin liners full of rubbish. He still couldn't hear anything other than the sound of his own quick, short breaths that he was trying to control, and the shuffling of his feet on the dusty floor.

The light up ahead looked like daylight making its way into the tunnel, rather than the artificial light of the bulbs.

When he got closer to the bin bags, even though it was still very dark, he realised they were moving, almost rustling, like they had someone or something inside.

The darkness was playing tricks on him. He stopped and stared at the shapes on the ground, trying hard to make out what they were. Keeping his feet completely still, he leaned his head down, trying to see, but also suddenly aware of a faint rustling sound. Philip was tempted to turn back, but if he did, he knew he'd want to come straight back down here. He had to keep going.

Suddenly, the dark shapes – no more than twenty feet away now – started to move. He saw three sets of eyes turn and look straight at him.

His heart stopped.

His breathing stopped.

The shapes suddenly jumped up from whatever they were doing and headed straight for him. It was as if they were gathered around something on the floor, almost like they were feeding.

Philip didn't stay to find out.

He turned and shot into a sprint, running faster than he'd ever ran before, dropping the mop handle as he went. He turned the dark corner, putting his hands on the wall to stop himself from running straight into it.

He could hear the scuffling sounds behind him as the creatures gave chase. They made noises, like 'Bah,' and 'Da,' not making sense, but more like screaming sounds, almost like chimpanzees.

He glanced back over his shoulder as he ran; he thought he saw three or four shapes chasing him in the dark. They again looked like Labradors, chasing him on all fours.

He ran and ran, ignoring the fact that his body wasn't up to a chase like this anymore. He held his breath as he finally reached the staircase. Stepping over Twisty, he ran up the steps quicker than he'd ever climbed steps in his life.

As he reached the top of the steps and entered the hallway, he slammed the door shut behind him and then quickly grabbed the armchair and dragged it across the floor, slamming it hard against the basement door.

He then threw himself into the chair, hoping the extra weight would stop his attackers from pushing the door open. He waited, expecting to hear the noise of the 'Labradors' climbing the steps and hitting the door, but it didn't happen.

He sat in the chair, breathing heavily, feeling both hot and cold at the same time. He didn't feel safe anymore. Maybe it was time to call the police, or maybe it was time to leave.

As he sat there recovering from his ordeal, Daisy wandered through from the living room, momentarily stopping to yawn. She came up to Philip and put her head on his knee, wanting to be stroked, obviously oblivious to the stressful situation that Philip had just endured.

Philip obliged and stroked her head, feeling his heart slow down as he did.

30

Philip spent the rest of the day aimlessly wandering around the house. He now knew for certain that something was down there, but he still didn't want to phone the police. He realised how ridiculous it would sound. *Hello, police? I have some creatures in my basement that steal from me and chase me around the house, occasionally knocking me down the stairs, could you send someone to investigate? Oh, and by the way, I'm a famous author who's lying low because of a recent indiscretion and attempted bribery.*

Philip knew how it would go. Not only because he'd once been a police officer, but also because he'd written many stories about the world of policing. Philip knew that the story would hit the newspapers the very next day if he was to call them out to his dilemma. His identity would also be revealed to the locals of Greysands. It wasn't imperative that he kept who he was a secret from the locals, but if Jade Romily revealed the footage to the world, it'd be much easier to walk around the town if nobody knew it was him.

He also didn't feel as though he could ask anyone else for help. He'd just lost Tom, partly because of the previous night's stress, he thought. He didn't want to put Charlotte through the same thing and risk her getting hurt or injured.

All these thoughts kept spinning around his head as he paced up and down the living room, occasionally stopping to admire the view, and occasionally letting Daisy outside through the kitchen door to let her use his back garden as a bathroom.

He just couldn't think of what to do next. One thing was for sure, he wasn't going to do any writing today, not after the events of the last twenty-four hours.

It was dark now, as he sat eating a sandwich at his desk, looking through the window at the shoreline.

He put the sandwich back on the plate and pushed it away from him as he leaned his elbows onto the desk and stared through the window as he sat in the dark room watching the waves in the distance move back and forth in the light from the streetlamp outside of his house, with the occasional spin of orange glow from the lighthouse ...

The lighthouse ...

The lighthouse was working, even though Tom was dead.

Philip stood and looked through the window at the tall building at the top of the hill. He couldn't see any movement at the top, other than the light of course. There wasn't anybody standing on the mezzanine balcony. This didn't mean that no one was in there. They could be in the kitchen or living area. But either way, he had to find out.

He put his coat and hat on and attached Daisy's lead to her collar and set off towards the lighthouse, locking his door as he left.

As he reached the lighthouse, before he could press the buzzer, the door opened.

He jumped back to see Councillor Fisher come through the door, dressed in a long winter coat, almost like the type a mafia boss would wear.

'Philip,' Councillor Fisher said, as he turned and locked

the door.

'Mr Fisher,' Philip said, still ignoring the title. 'I was wondering who was running the lighthouse.'

'Well, Tom never let an evening go by without the light shining across the bay. Even when he was ill with the flu, he'd still make his way here. I couldn't let his good work go to waste, could I?'

'I suppose not,' Philip said. Perhaps the councillor wasn't the monster people made him out to be, he thought. Although a man like Councillor Fisher was all about image. He might be doing a nice thing for Tom, but he sure as hell would make sure everyone knew about it.

'Terrible losing him like that. The town won't be the same without him,' Fisher said.

'I'm sure it won't. Listen, have you got five minutes for a chat? I'd like to discuss something with you.'

'No problem,' Councillor Fisher said. 'But not out here; it's freezing.'

'Come to the house,' Philip said.

They both then set off through the snow.

31

They sat at the kitchen table as Philip poured them each a glass of Tom's whisky.

Daisy wandered through to the living room and jumped up onto the sofa. She was already making herself at home, he thought.

'I never had you down as a scotch drinker, Philip,' he said, smelling the glass as if he was at a wine tasting.

Philip didn't know why, but everything this man did seemed to infuriate him. Everything he did was pretentious; the way he always wore a suit, always used his title, and now he was a whisky expert too.

Councillor Fisher winced as he took a sip, so perhaps he wasn't an expert after all.

'I'm not usually, but this is Tom's whisky. He brought it over last night. Seems fitting that we would lift a glass in his honour, don't you think?'

'Indeed,' Fisher said, raising his glass to clink with Philip's.

Philip obliged.

'So, what would you like to discuss with me?' he said, sounding official, as though it was a council board meeting.

'Do we know anything about how Tom died?'

'The cause of death hasn't been confirmed as of yet. Charlotte found him this morning lying on the floor in his hallway with the door open. I believe the central heating was pumping heat out all night, but it's still possible he collapsed but then died of the cold. Even though he was lying next to his radiator, it would still be freezing cold with the door open.'

'Do you think it could have been a heart attack?' Philip asked.

Fisher took another sip of whisky. 'Tom wasn't the healthiest of gentlemen; not since his wife passed away. He was keeping the chip shop going on his own with his regular custom, put it that way. And he liked a drink of course.'

Philip nodded. He couldn't blame Tom for drinking to excess and not eating properly. Losing your life-partner must be hard to cope with. Tom seemed like a strong man on the outside, but you never knew what was going on with someone on the inside.

'I didn't know he'd been spending evenings with you, though,' Fisher said.

'Just a couple of pints one night in the pub, and a chippy supper on another night. I haven't yet been here a week, don't forget.'

'Of course.'

'Although it's starting to feel like I've been here for months.'

'Why so?'

Philip took a sip as he thought about how this might be a good point to steer the conversation towards the events since he'd arrived in the town. 'It's been an odd week I suppose. I'm falling in love with this little town, but it's a very strange place that's taking some getting used to.'

'Well, I'm sure you'll get used to it. It's a town with a big heart. It just needs a little more guidance, that's all. We'll soon have the visitors coming back to us; you'll see.'

Philip didn't want to get into another discussion about the situation of this dying and desolate seaside town. Although he was interested in its welfare and did hope it would start to grow, at that moment he was more interested in the creatures that lived in his basement. He'd also noticed that Councillor Fisher hadn't asked why there was an armchair pushed up against the basement door, even though he had to walk sideways to get past it.

Philip was wondering if this man already knew about the strange goings-on in the park house.

'I wanted to talk to you about something,' Philip said, before taking another sip of whisky.

'Of course.'

He then had a quick change of mind. 'Actually, I'd like to show you something.'

Fisher nodded, looking intrigued.

'I'd like you to come down into the basement with me.'

Fisher's demeanour suddenly changed. He tried to hide his obvious discomfort, but Philip was trained to look for these little nuances in people's behaviour. He was uncomfortable, but trying his best to look relaxed.

'Why would I need to go into your basement?'

'I'd just like to show you what's down there.'

'Philip, I used to own this house. I'm very aware of what's down there.'

'And what is it that's down there?' *Other than a creepy-looking clown that's now sitting at the bottom of the steps.*

'It's just boxes of old junk and supplies from the amusement park. Nothing more.'

'And the tunnel?'

'Tunnel? What about it?'

'You're aware that there's a tunnel that leads to the park?'

'Of course I am. My family owned the park. I'm very aware

that there's an underground entrance to the park. It's nothing unusual. It was used to move supplies back and forth from the house.'

'And?'

'And what?'

'What else is down there?'

He looked at his watch. 'Look, Philip, I could do with making a move. I have things to sort out.'

'What about the creatures?'

There it was. He'd said it. He felt stupid saying it, but it was out there now and it stopped Councillor Fisher as he'd started to get up from his seat.

'Creatures?'

Philip nodded.

Councillor Fisher stood and gently placed the chair under the table.

'Philip, I think you've been reading too many science fiction novels.'

Before Philip could answer, there was a knock at the door. Philip could see the relief on Fisher's face.

Philip thought of ignoring the door and continuing to press Fisher about the knowledge he might have about the creatures in his basement. But he also thought about whoever it was at his front door standing in the cold.

He decided to go and open it, hoping to get rid of whoever it was and carry on with his discussion. But his intentions changed as he opened the door and saw Charlotte standing there in her winter coat and hat. Judging from the redness around her eyes she'd been crying very recently.

'Charlotte, come in,' he said, standing aside. 'I'm very sorry about Tom.'

As she walked in, Councillor Fisher walked past them towards the door, putting his coat on as he did.

'Hello, Charlotte,' he said, rubbing her shoulder. 'Stay strong. Tom wouldn't want to see you upset.'

She nodded, wiping her nose with a tissue.

'Thanks for the drink, Philip.'

'I'd like to finish our conversation at some point.'

'Anytime,' he said, walking away. 'Lock your doors.'

With that, he'd left the path and headed off down the road.

Lock your doors? Philip thought. Not much point if there's an underground tunnel leading into your house.

Philip now wanted to find out more about Tom, and he wanted to check that Charlotte was OK. Finding out if the councillor knew anything about the creatures in the basement was going to have to wait for another day.

32

Philip did the typical English thing to help people in times of crises and distress; he made her a cup of tea. They sat on the sofa in the living room with Daisy lying between them. Philip had switched his desk lamp on to brighten the room a little. Charlotte wasn't crying like before, but her eyes were still wet and she still held a crumpled tissue in her hand.

'I'm guessing you and Tom were good friends,' Philip said.

'More like family, really,' she said. 'He and my dad worked together years ago. He comes to my house every year for Christmas.'

Philip noticed she still spoke of Tom in the present tense. He understood why and had no intentions of correcting her.

'Obviously it's been just the two of us in recent years. This place won't be the same without him.' She turned to look at Daisy as she stroked her. 'And I don't know where this little thing is going to end up. I work most evenings in the pub.'

'Well she can stay here until you decide what's best,' Philip said, still influenced by the guilt of possibly assisting Tom towards an early grave. He had a dog as a child so he knew how to look after them, but a dog was a long-term commitment that he shouldn't really be taking on with his life still up in the air. He didn't know how long he'd be staying in Greysands and he didn't know where he would be six months from now. He had a twelve-month lease on the house, but that didn't mean he had to stay in it for the full year; although at that moment, being in the company of Charlotte once more, he didn't want to be anywhere else.

'Thank you, Philip. She seems to like you.'

Philip didn't know why she thought that but he didn't question it. They spent the next hour or so talking, mainly about Tom and what would happen to the lighthouse, and about the funeral arrangements. Charlotte was just thinking out loud, Philip thought. So, he just sat there and listened to her talk.

There was a knock at the door.

Daisy jumped up first to see who it was.

Philip walked through the doorway to the hall before opening the front door.

His heart sank as he found Lesley on the other side of it, dressed in her expensive winter coat. Philip noticed Daniel's car parked at the end of the driveway.

Daniel waved but obviously had no intentions of coming into the house. Today he was clearly just a chauffeur for Lesley.

Lesley walked past Philip without waiting to be invited in.

'Right, I've decided we'll talk about things but I'm not going to leave Daniel waiting too long so we'll have to get straight to it and no flannel ...' she stopped mid-sentence as she entered the living room. She'd looked down and saw Daisy following her. 'Whose dog is this?' she asked. But as she looked up from the little grey and white whippet, she saw Charlotte getting up from the sofa.

The silence seemed to go on forever as she stared at Charlotte. Daniel had met Charlotte briefly the other day, but Philip didn't imagine he'd have told Lesley about her.

Lesley moved her jaw from side to side. She looked angrier than he'd ever seen her before.

'And who's *this*?' Lesley demanded, looking at Charlotte as she might have done if she'd stepped in something Daisy had left on the floor.

'This is Charlotte,' Philip said. 'She's a friend from the area. A good friend of hers died ...'

Lesley cut him off. 'Oh, another "friend", eh?'

'Lesley ...'

'You seem to be good at making new friends all of a sudden.'

'I'll go ...' Charlotte started to say.

'No!' Lesley cried. 'It's fine. You stay, love. You look a bit young for him but you're welcome to him!' She then stepped towards Philip. 'To think I actually came here to sort things out and maybe give you another chance! What a fool I was!' She shook her head slowly.

'Lesley, you have to listen ...'

'I have to go, Philip. That's what I have to do; go. You won't see me again. You enjoy your new life here. I hope you're very happy.'

With that, she walked out, slamming the door behind her.

Charlotte was red-faced. She walked through to the hallway and put her coat and hat on.

'Charlotte, you don't have to ...'

'Goodbye, Philip,' she said, and then left, not slamming the door as hard as Lesley did, but hard enough for Philip to know she wasn't happy.

He looked down at Daisy. As her soft brown eyes gazed back up at him, he thought that at that moment, she was his only friend.

33

For the next six days Philip kept himself to himself. Charlotte hadn't been to see him since the uncomfortable visit from Lesley, and who could blame her? Lesley had a vicious look on her face when she was angry, no more so than that night.

Charlotte was obviously embarrassed and a little unnerved by the situation and hadn't really spoken to Philip since. He thought they were becoming close; close enough to maybe even become an item. Age didn't seem to be a factor when they were together. When he was with her, he felt young again. But Lesley's outburst – albeit an understandable one without knowing the true facts – seemed to put an end to Charlotte's interest in Philip. He'd been to the pub a couple of times, but she just served him in her usual polite way. Only, unlike previous nights in the pub, she never came over to his table to speak to him.

After feeling the brush-off from Charlotte, and obviously not having Tom to drink with any more, Philip just stayed at home. He also decided to keep out of people's way because of not knowing how Tom had died. He still felt responsible. Even though it was obvious that Tom wasn't a very healthy man, the night they kept a vigil in his house must've contributed to his death. Philip had almost fully convinced himself of this by now.

After drinking more of Tom's whisky one night, he took a large kitchen knife into the basement. He even let Daisy follow him down there. But when he got as far as he was when he saw the creatures last time, he turned back. He considered going through the open area that let the light in, and into the park, but without anyone to help him, he lost his nerve and went back to the house. Although he didn't see the creatures, he still pushed the armchair back in front of the basement door, and that's where it stayed.

The one benefit to keeping himself locked away from the rest of the town was how much writing he'd managed to do. He never decided how long a first draft would be before writing it. He always made a point of letting the story go where it went. Most of his earlier novels were around the three-hundred-page mark. His more recent ones were five hundred plus. This one was looking like it could end up a seven-hundred-page book, and every page of it necessary to the story. He was pretty certain he was on the home stretch. He'd just revealed to the reader who the killer was, which he hoped nobody would've guessed by this point, so he knew he was almost there.

Philip used to judge how good the ending was by letting Lesley read the manuscript in full from start to finish. He would draw a red line across the page at the point where the ending was about to be revealed. At that point she would come to him and try to guess what happened. If she guessed correctly, then he had to think again. If she was surprised, then his work was done; except for another three or four months of editing that was.

He wondered if he should tell Charlotte about his career and try to get her to read the draft. He really enjoyed the fact that nobody knew who he was in this town, especially since the incident with the woman from the hotel. But maybe if he could get Charlotte to talk to him again, he could let her in on his secret. He already knew she liked to read, so she might be useful to him.

It seemed to Philip that Daisy was becoming a permanent member of his family. He'd been to Karen's to buy more dog food and she didn't talk about Daisy as if it was a temporary arrangement. He didn't mind really. In fact, he quite liked having some company and wondered why he hadn't got himself a little canine friend before.

He found having a dog a great way of having a break from writing while he gathered his thoughts. Stepping away from his laptop to let her out in the garden or walking her along the seafront was a great way of getting his head together before embarking on the next stretch of writing.

Philip was still happy – apart from the whatever was happening in his basement – living in this unusual, interesting town. He certainly didn't want to go back to Chorley after his visit from Lesley. He just felt as though he needed to start again, in his own life but also in Greysands. He wanted to let the mourning for Tom disperse a little before trying to make friends again with the locals. He also wanted to finish talking to Councillor Fisher. He was certain that he knew more than he was letting on. Things had gone quiet the last week with regards to the disturbances. But he knew he hadn't imagined it, and he knew he hadn't seen the last of them.

34

It was almost ten-thirty in the evening when Philip stepped out of his front door with Daisy by his side. The snow was receding by now, revealing the grey path heading from the house to the front gate. The snow had melted from his car; he wondered if it would even start. He'd been in Greysands for eleven days by now and not driven since moving to the town. It crossed his mind whether he'd remember how to drive when the time came to go anywhere.

He walked along the seafront on the opposite side of the road to the pub. He contemplated going inside for a pint, but he didn't really feel like being ignored by Charlotte. He'd spent a lot of time over the last few days trying to work out what the best course of action to take was.

He wondered if he should try to reconcile with Lesley. The more time went by, the more he thought he didn't want to stay married to her. He felt as though his marriage was dead. But he also felt as though trying to save it was the right thing to do. But why? Was it for Lesley's sake, or for his fans, the people who bought his books? He wondered if he'd lose any credibility from the literary world for failing at his marriage, even if the Jade Romily situation stayed a secret.

Was he just trying to save his marriage for the sake of not being thought of as a failure? The more he thought about it, the more he wanted to let his marriage come to an end. The last week in Greysands had taken a turn for the worse, but he still loved the place and he still wanted to stay. He hoped he could convince Charlotte to give him another chance. He didn't really think he'd done anything wrong; he'd just allowed Charlotte to fall into an embarrassing and awkward situation. He understood that she wouldn't have appreciated being thought of as *the other woman* in an argument between a man and his wife, but it wasn't Philip's fault that Lesley turned up unannounced. But he did think that maybe he could've handled it better.

He decided he'd go and speak to Charlotte, but as he turned to cross the road, he saw her come through the door of the pub. She walked over to him, arms folded, wearing a jumper but no coat.

'Charlotte,' Philip said.

'It's Tom's funeral tomorrow,' she handed him a piece of paper with an address scribbled on it. 'That's the church. Be there for one-thirty if you're coming, and back here afterwards for the wake.'

'Of course, I'll be there,' he said. 'Can I help in any way, or give anyone a lift?'

She'd already turned to go inside, but then stopped before she opened the door.

She then turned to face Philip before saying, 'Just bring Daisy. Tom would've wanted her there.'

'Do they let dogs ...' before he could finish his sentence, she'd gone back into the pub.

It was a start, he thought. At least he was invited to the funeral, even if it was only because he was Daisy's plus one. Maybe the wake would be a good place to sit down with Charlotte and try to make up. He thought they were on the verge of a romantic relationship, in spite of the age difference.

He thought of her as more than a friend, and knew she saw him in the same way. He'd read signals from women throughout his years and he knew enough to know this was more than just friendship. And she wouldn't be so annoyed if she had no intentions of taking things further with him.

He hoped that somehow, he could rebuild the bridge between them.

35

The church was a mile or so from Philip's house so he decided to drive there. The snow was slowly but surely melting, even though it didn't feel any warmer than it had been during the previous weeks in Greysands. After starting the engine – he'd already tried early that morning to make sure it still worked – he set off in plenty of time to get there before the service started.

The church was around half full, which Philip thought was about right for the amount of people who lived in Greysands. He sat in a pew in the middle of the church, which left him a row behind everyone else. The local fishermen were the pall-bearers. Karen, Councillor Fisher and Charlotte all sat in the front row, with some other people, maybe Tom's friends or distant relatives. Behind them, there were another couple of locals who Philip hadn't met properly, but thought he'd seen their faces before, most likely in the pub.

Daisy was oblivious to what was going on. She whimpered through most of the service, causing the people in front to turn and look at her with a pitiful expression as though they thought she was crying for her owner. Philip was sure that Daisy was upset at losing her master; after all, she'd lain with him all night the night he died. But the friends of Tom Dawson presumed the dog was crying because she was at her master's funeral, whereas Philip knew full well she was crying because of how bloody cold the church was.

The vicar droned on for half an hour, sporadically stopping for the odd hymn, each played at several different tempos by the organist who must've been the other side of ninety if he was a day.

Philip didn't learn much about Tom from the sermon that he hadn't heard from Tom himself when he was alive; except for how he had a short time as a professional footballer, and was even on the books at Blackpool F.C. before having to retire early with a knee injury. Tom hadn't told him about that part of his life.

Philip thought he'd search the Internet to see if he was there long enough for his name to be in the history books. But he thought it was more likely that he'd just had a trial there or maybe even spent a year or so in the reserves. Anything more than that and he'd have mentioned it to him when they were telling each other their life stories over the bottle of whisky.

Philip thought the service was coming to an end when the Reverend asked if anyone would like to say a few words. Philip hoped that Charlotte would speak, but unfortunately, it was Councillor Fisher who jumped out of his seat as though a mild electrical current had suddenly shot through the cold, hard, wooden bench.

He stood behind the pulpit in his black suit and tie, leaning on the wooden frame as though he was Donald Trump about to give an address to his public.

Philip tried not to shake his head.

'Well,' he started. 'Our little town has just lost a huge character, a character who will never be replaced. We have all known Tom for most, if not all, of our lives. He was a simple man with simple hopes and dreams. All he wanted was to live in

Greysands with his wife Betty, and his pet dog, Daisy. He loved this town so much that he fought tooth and nail to keep the lighthouse going, even working there every night for free. And I know he was retired and you could say "so what, it kept him busy," but not everyone would give up their free time every single night, come rain, sleet or snow. And it isn't as simple as him just turning a switch on and off, he also did all the maintenance and upkeep of the building himself.'

Philip was starting to think that maybe the councillor wasn't going to make his speech about himself after all.

'I think that we can all agree that today is a very sad day for our town. Although we sometimes have our differences, we all need to pull together and look after each other. People deal with death in different ways. Some of us are finding it harder than others. But if we all look out for each other, pick up the phone, knock on your neighbour's door, put your hand on a friend's shoulder, we can all cope with this loss and learn to carry on.'

He's still doing OK, Philip thought.

'I know that *I* for one am going to miss him terribly. I'll miss our chats, I'll miss knowing he's up in the lighthouse, I'll even miss the little arguments we occasionally had.'

There was a slight titter from the congregation at this.

Councillor Fisher was doing a pretty good job with his speech, even winning Philip over a little.

'But…' Fisher's voice suddenly broke as he almost began to cry. He put his head down and stared at the floor as he gathered himself.

'But at least he's with Betty now,' he finished, in a slightly croaky voice. There was no acting. Councillor Fisher was genuinely upset at losing Tom. Perhaps there was more to their relationship than Tom had let on. Tom definitely didn't show any love for Councillor Fisher, but perhaps there had been a friendship somewhere along the line.

36

After dropping his Mercedes off at home, Philip walked to the pub with Daisy. He didn't speak to anyone at the funeral but to be fair, nobody was really talking. They all acknowledged each other with eye contact and a slight nod of the head, but Philip could see that everyone who attended Tom's funeral had a lump in their throat.

As he walked through the door of the pub he was greeted by a very different atmosphere. The pub was packed with people. In the corner – the corner that Philip now thought of as his regular spot – the table was pushed further into the centre of the room because three men and a woman were sat there playing a song and singing loudly.

The bearded man closest to the door was playing an acoustic guitar, as was the man next to him. The woman was playing a violin and the man on the end, the ukulele. As Philip walked through the crowd of people with Daisy, everyone nodded to him as they sang along to the folk band.

The locals seemed a lot friendlier towards him than they were the first time he came into this pub. Perhaps the loss of a local brought out the good in everyone. He thought of them as nice people, but he didn't feel welcomed by them; but today there was a much happier feeling to the place; which he found surprising considering the occasion. Maybe he was winning them over simply because he seemed to have adopted Daisy, even though he didn't remember offering to.

He couldn't see Charlotte anywhere, so he ordered his pint of bitter from the landlord. He picked up his drink and went to sit on a bar stool at the opposite end of the bar. He still felt part of the group, but was a little more comfortable on the edge of the room and not in the middle of the crowd. Partly because of not knowing everybody, but also because he didn't feel as though he officially qualified as one of the mourners. Yes, he knew Tom, and yes, he was becoming friends with him, but he was still an outsider, and he was possibly partly to blame for Tom's death.

Philip was trying to work out where he'd heard the folk song before. It sounded like an old English country song, almost a sea chanty. Then it hit him. It was Mark Knopfler's 'Haul Away'. Philip didn't get the chance to listen to music very often, but he liked to listen to Mark Knopfler whenever he had to drive anywhere. He found it relaxed him so he didn't get as annoyed when drivers pulled out on him without indicating, or slammed on brakes and turned at the last minute. Driving was the one thing that would always get him angry. Listening to the soothing tones of Mr Knopfler's country songs – mostly stories about the sea – helped him turn a blind eye to other people's stupidity.

He quietly sang along, '*Our lucky ship, speeds across the sea. I'm a living man, and you're a cold one.*'

As the song finished, the group went straight into another one, this time one that Philip didn't know. He was still enjoying listening to them, but he wondered whether they'd be playing all night. He thought it was an interesting way to deal with the loss of one of their own; why shouldn't they play music and turn the wake into a party? The serious part was left at the church, and now it was time to have a drink and celebrate Tom's life. People should learn from Greysands, he thought. The English have a stiff-upper-lipped way of handling things like funerals. Other cultures celebrate death as though it's part of life. Philip didn't think there was anything wrong with that at all.

Charlotte appeared from behind the bar. She crouched down to stroke Daisy and said a quick hello to Philip, but then stood and walked back behind the bar. She didn't smile the beautiful smile that she used to greet him with. It was more of a forced clenching of the lips, the kind you'd use if someone stepped out of your way as you passed them on the street.

Philip decided he was going to go and speak to her and tell her he was sorry again, but before he could stand, an older gentleman sat down next to him.

'Wonderful service, don't you think?' he asked while stroking Daisy with one hand and holding a pint in the other.

'Yes,' Philip said. 'It was a very nice service; very moving.'

'I'm Richard,' the man said, as he offered his hand.

'Philip,' he said, shaking it.

He spoke to Richard for about an hour, and more people gathered around as they talked. They weren't talking about anything overly intellectual. It was just simple pub talk. As the evening went on, Philip felt more and more at ease with the locals, but what he wanted to do was to speak to Charlotte. However, that wasn't looking as though it was going to happen.

Hours later, as the evening drew to a close and the pub slowly began to empty, Philip was feeling the alcohol spinning around in his head. He wasn't drunk as such, but he was definitely feeling as though he was under the influence.

Charlotte and the landlord – whose name Philip still didn't know – were sitting on stools in front of the bar. Philip was at the left of the bar at one of the tables with Daisy on the floor at his feet. The old man from the cafe, Gerald he thought his name was, was opposite him at a table on the other side of the pub, with Karen one table along. And Councillor Fisher was at the table to Philip's right. Everyone was spread out, but with the pub almost empty, they were all talking with each other, mostly about Tom. But then the landlord decided to change the subject.

'So, Philip. What brought you to our little town?'

He thought for a moment. He didn't want his alcohol-filled brain to suddenly start telling stories of his marriage breakdown or the Jade Romily incident.

'I just fancied a new start, that's all.'

'I was thinking,' Councillor Fisher started, 'Charlotte told me you work from home.'

'Yes,' Philip said.

'Well, I was wondering if you fancied taking over Tom's job at the lighthouse?'

This surprised Philip, partly because Fisher had asked him, but mostly at how excited he was at the thought of running the lighthouse. Police constable to writer to lighthouse keeper didn't seem like a usual progression in one's career, but for some reason, he could really see himself doing it.

'I say job,' Fisher added. 'It's volunteer work really. But it isn't difficult. You just sit around doing nothing for most of the time. Maybe that would suit you working from home. And your house is but fifty yards from the lighthouse.'

Philip gave a little nod. 'I like the idea, certainly. But let me sleep on it.'

He wondered if taking on the role would cement his position in the town permanently. But he definitely liked the idea. He just didn't want to agree to something like that while under the influence of several pints of bitter.

'So how long am I going to have Daisy living with me?' he asked.

'She seems to like you,' Charlotte said, speaking to him for the first time since most of the regulars left the pub.

'It's just that I don't remember anyone asking me if I wanted to adopt a dog.'

'We all pull together around here,' Gerald said, from the other side of the room. 'But I don't know why she was given to you, with you being an outsider.'

Philip was confused. 'Why should that matter?'

'Most people who come here don't last very long,' Gerald said, not looking up from his pint.

'Gerald,' Karen said, quietly, stopping him from talking.

'It's OK, Karen,' Philip said. 'I'm very aware that this town has secrets that it doesn't want to share with the newcomers.'

He saw them all glance at each other.

Nobody spoke again for a moment; an uncomfortable moment, Philip thought.

After a minute or so went by, Charlotte got up and headed towards the lavatories.

Karen then started a conversation about the church service, and how difficult, but how lovely it was.

Philip saw a chance to speak to Charlotte and headed for the lavatories himself.

After a moment or two of pacing the floor outside the doors, while he listened to the voices in the other room talking about Tom, Charlotte finally came through the door.

She jumped as she came through the doorway and saw Philip.

He put his hands up to show he didn't mean to scare her.

'Sorry, I just want to talk.'

'Well, I don't want to talk to you,' she said, trying to push past him.

He stepped in front of her again. 'Please, Charlotte. Look, I know you're upset but ...'

'Upset?' she said loudly, but not loud enough to be heard in the bar, he hoped.

'I'm more than upset. It was humiliating. I've never been accused of being the other woman before. It felt so sordid. I would never do that.'

'I know you wouldn't. She got the wrong end of the stick, that's all.'

Charlotte stopped and stared at him. 'You don't get it do you?'

'Get what?'

She shook her head. 'I actually liked you,' she said. 'I was falling for you. But then I find out that you're still an item with your wife.'

'What? No. We're not together. We're separated and there's no going back.'

'Well, why did you protest so much to her that you and I were just friends?'

That question stopped him in his tracks. He didn't know the answer. Was it to keep the peace? Was it because he really wanted to save his marriage? Was it so Lesley wouldn't lose her temper even more than she had? He didn't know.

Charlotte seemed to calm down a little. She stepped towards him and said, 'Look, I really like you. But I can't get involved in someone's marriage, especially someone whose private life could be all over the newspapers.'

Philip stood aghast at what he'd just heard Charlotte say.

He just stared at her as he tried to make sense of her statement.

'What did you say?'

'I said I can't get involved ...'

'No. The part about newspapers.'

'I'm sure your divorce will hit the headlines, won't it?'

He shook his head. 'Are you saying you know who I am?'

'Of course. You're Philip Lloyd, the novelist. I have most of your books at home.'

Philip walked away and stood with his back against the wall.

'What's the problem?' Charlotte asked.

'I didn't think anyone knew who I was. I was trying to keep it a secret while I sorted my life out.'

'Oh, don't worry; nobody else knows.'

'Really?'

'Yes. Oh, Karen knows. But that's it, I think. I got the impression you wanted to stay incognito so we said we wouldn't tell anyone.'

Philip laughed. 'This town *is* good at keeping secrets, isn't it?'

Charlotte took a step forward so she was standing right in front of him. 'Look. I'm not interested in money. With what I earn at the pub I get by OK, and I've no desire to leave Greysands. Plus, I have quite a large bank balance through my dad's inheritance, so trust me when I say, I'm not interested in you for your money.'

'I didn't think you ...'

'I know there's an age difference between us, but I think we could work; or at least I thought we could.'

'I think we could ...'

'But,' she said, raising her finger to stop him from talking, 'I didn't see a man who wanted to end his marriage that night. I saw a man who was trying his best to save his marriage.'

'That's not true ...'

'Look, this is what I have to say, so you listen,' Charlotte said, sternly.

So far Philip had only seen the mild-mannered and gentle version of Charlotte. This version of her was very strict, almost like a schoolteacher.

'OK,' he said.

'I want you to go to your wife. Leave Daisy with me and go and see her tomorrow. Try to work things out or try to bring it to an end. If I don't see you again, then that's fine. At least I won't get caught up in the media side of things. But if you end it and end it properly, I'll be here.'

The whole conversation left him unable to speak. He was still reeling from the fact that Charlotte not only knew who he was, but had kept it from everyone else in the town. He now liked her even more, but he was confused. He'd been married for a long time. He knew that Charlotte was right. He had to end things properly. All he'd been doing for the last few weeks was hiding from his problems.

Charlotte looked him in the eye. 'Your choice,' she said, before briskly walking away.

Philip stood where he was, completely perplexed by Charlotte's dressing-down. He suddenly felt sober. He heard

Charlotte say goodnight to the landlord, Gerald, Karen and Councillor Fisher.

He walked back through to the bar area and sat at his table.

'Why has Charlotte taken Daisy?' Councillor Fisher asked.

'Erm… I have to drive somewhere tomorrow. I asked her if she'd take her for the day.'

The landlord got them all a shot of whisky and they sat around talking in the low light of the quiet, almost empty pub.

Philip dusted himself off from Charlotte's scolding and allowed the conversation to flow once more. But as the drink got hold of him again, he decided he wanted to know more about the town and the strange occurrences, so he waited until the conversation stopped and then said, 'So are you four like the town elders then?'

They all looked at each other, confusion on their faces.

'What do you mean?' Karen said.

'Is it just you that knows the truth about what goes on here, or does everybody know?'

'Philip,' Fisher said. 'Come on, let's let sleeping dogs lie.'

Philip laughed. 'Sleeping dogs? I can't let sleeping dogs lie because they keep waking me up and disturbing me.'

There was a silence.

'Don't you think I have a right to know?'

'Aye,' Gerald said in agreement.

'Gerald,' Karen snapped under her breath.

'Well he has.'

Another long silence followed.

'I suppose I'll just have to wait until I've been here long enough to be thought of as a local.'

'Hmm, you'll be waiting a long time,' Gerald said.

'There aren't any secrets, Philip. We're just a quiet little seaside town that keeps itself to itself,' Karen said.

Gerald gave a quiet laugh that made his shoulders bounce a little.

Philip could see that Gerald's comments had the others on edge. He wondered if he could keep pressing to see whether Gerald would say more.

'Don't worry,' Philip said. 'I'll find out sooner or later.'

'Find out what?' Fisher said.

'What it is you're all hiding, why you tell each other to lock your doors all the time and what's going on in my house.'

'There's nothing going on,' Fisher said. 'It's an old house that creeks and settles.'

Philip laughed; so did Gerald.

'Whatever it is wandering around my basement, it's nothing to do with creaking or settling.'

The alcohol was kicking in, Philip thought.

'It's coming up to the full moon,' Gerald said, still staring at his pint. 'That's when the howling starts ...'

'All right,' the landlord shouted, jumping off his seat. 'Time to close up everyone.'

'No,' Philip shouted. 'What howling?'

The landlord dropped his shoulders and shook his head. 'I really need to close up,' he said quietly.

Philip didn't move. He turned his gaze to Gerald on the other side of the room. 'Howling?'

Gerald didn't answer. He swallowed the last of his drink and then got out of his seat and headed for the door.

'You'll see,' he said quietly as he left.

Philip felt like a police officer again, trying to get the truth from people who were all aware of what was really going on. He didn't want to leave it there. He wanted to continue.

'I need to know what's going on,' he said. He looked at each of the faces left in the room. The landlord stared at the floor. Karen seemed to look at him with a pitiful expression. Councillor Fisher looked him in the eye, but he had an expression of guilt and uneasiness.

Philip waited for an answer.

It didn't come.

He felt more and more frustrated by their refusal to tell him the truth. He got up from his seat, then drank the whisky that was left in his glass before slamming in down on the table, almost hard enough to break it.

'You know what; I'm done,' he said, heading for the door. 'If you're all going to keep secrets then I'm going to have to deal with things head on.'

'Let's just settle ...' Fisher began, but Philip cut him off.

'No!' he snapped. 'I'm sick of this. I'm going into that basement and I'm going to take the largest kitchen knife I have and I'm going to deal with it once and for all.'

He left the pub, letting the door swing shut behind him. He didn't know if he was behaving like this because he'd had a few too many to drink, or whether he was just at the end of his tether. Either way, he was angry and he was going to go into the basement, that he was sure of.

37

Philip rummaged through the kitchen drawer for a knife. He found several, but the one he took out was at least ten inches long. It was old and looked a little rust-stained, but it would do just fine. He slammed the drawer shut and opened the bottom cupboard, taking out the torch he'd put there earlier; he'd remembered it was in the car when he was driving to the funeral, so had brought it inside afterwards. It would've been useful if he'd remembered it when the power first went out, especially when he and Tom went into the basement. He then went over to the armchair that was still blocking the door to the basement. After pushing it aside and opening the door, he lit the torch, held the knife in his right hand, blade pointing downwards ready for action, and headed down the steps.

Back at the pub his anger and alcohol intake had taken over him. Now, as he descended the creaky wooden staircase, lit by his torch and a single low wattage bulb above the bottom of the steps, he suddenly felt very scared. Partly because of dealing with the creatures again, but also because of a fear of his own actions.

He knew losing his temper could get him into trouble, but he'd had enough. If the *elders* of the town wouldn't tell him what was happening, then he needed to face it head on. The thing that made him more nervous than before was Gerald's mention of howling. Was he dealing with wolves, or possibly werewolves? As he made his way down the steps these thoughts were making his heart beat harder and harder. No amount of beer was going to take away the fear from the situation he'd got himself into.

If only he could go back to the night when he'd met Jade Romily, or whatever her name was. One stupid mistake had caused an avalanche of events that had brought him to where he was now. He couldn't help but love the town, and he was falling for Charlotte more and more. But he couldn't help thinking that if he'd done the right thing all those weeks ago, things would be as they were before. He'd be at his desk in his big house, writing, while overlooking his huge garden with the tennis court he hadn't used since the first month of moving in.

Things were very different now, he thought; very different.

As he got to the bottom of the steps, the cold maze of basement corridors was waiting for him. He felt his head swim from the alcohol. His fear was rising, but his determination to find the creatures and get an answer was higher than ever. He didn't necessarily feel as though he wanted to kill whatever they were, but he wasn't prepared to go into the basement unarmed.

Philip turned left at the bottom of the steps and walked slowly by the rooms he'd previously investigated, glancing inside each one. As he did, his heart almost stopped. Sat in the corner of the room, staring back at him, was Twisty the clown. Philip had forgotten all about him after dropping him at the foot of the steps. And now, the clown was back in the room where he originally was.

Philip walked over to Twisty, half-expecting him to move, and picked him up. He checked him over, but there was nothing different – he was still just a stuffed toy. A weird, creepy, stuffed toy that would give any sane child nightmares.

He put Twisty back on the chair and carried on with his journey.

He reached the mouth of the long corridor and walked slowly down the long, straight, alleyway, the occasional dim bulb lighting its own small area. He had his torch in one hand, knife in the other, but he still stepped slowly, allowing his eyes to adjust every time he entered a dark patch between the lights.

Nothing met him during this slow walk towards the turn at the end of the alleyway. When he reached the turn that headed left, he slowed down and tried to look around the corner first. He was wondering if he'd see the gaggle of creatures feasting on something like he did the last time. They chased him out then, but they wouldn't this time, he thought. He was going to stand his ground.

There was nothing up ahead as he went around the bend; at least nothing he could see. There were no more lights hanging from the ceiling from this point onwards. He remembered daylight shining through from the right-hand side of the tunnel, about twenty feet ahead of him. But now it was dark outside so this wasn't the case. He could feel the air getting much colder the further he walked, but still no creatures.

As he got to the spot where he'd last seen them, he had to decide which way to go. He could see the opening. It was two wooden doors that opened outwards with ten or so concrete steps leading up to the outside. But he could also choose to keep walking through the seemingly-endless corridor. Even though he'd only walked about fifty feet or so, his slow pace and watching out for the creatures, made it feel as though he'd walked a mile.

He shone the torch further into the corridor, but all he

could see were more red bricks continuing into the darkness. He decided to turn right and climb the steps to the outside.

The cold hit him even more as he reached the top of the steps. He was still wearing the winter coat he'd worn for the funeral, but it didn't stop him from shivering.

Philip looked around at the empty and decaying amusement park. The snow had partly melted from all the rides, but most of the grassed areas were still covered. The pathways were all but clear. He could see a little because the orange glow of the streetlights reached the park, even though there were shadows cast from his house and the surrounding fences. The lighthouse was still sending its light across the sea, but this didn't really help Philip's vision from his position at the back of the house.

Still holding the torch and knife, he walked through the park, moving the stream of light from the torch from side to side. He walked along the pathway past the pond where the swan-shaped pedalos resided. Although it was dark, he could see how dirty they were, and the muddy smell of the stale pond filled the air. It was obviously a man-made pond, but there clearly wasn't a filter or much in the way of plant life to keep the water clean.

Philip reached the dilapidated shed at the side of the pond, pushed the door open and shone his torch inside, holding the knife above his shoulder, ready to strike if need be. But there was only a broken shelf, which he presumed was once a counter for taking payments for the pedalos. Other than that, it was empty.

As he walked along the path, he reached the rollercoaster. It was reasonably large, especially for such a small amusement park, but it didn't look as though it'd been used in the last decade. As he shone his torch up at the tracks, he could see several old birds' nests along the rusty framework that spiralled above the park.

After examining the rollercoaster, Philip continued on his journey through the park. He walked by several different rides and stalls before he came to a large circular, glass building; perhaps once a gift shop or maybe a cafe. He walked over to the two doors at the front. They were dirty and cracked and he couldn't really see through into the building, especially as it was dark.

He pushed the doors open.

As he looked into the dark and dusty room, he wondered if he was making a mistake, wandering around in the dark. But he wasn't turning back now, even though fear was having a sobering effect. Maybe embarking on this mission had been a stupid idea.

The room smelled of damp. He couldn't see much as he spun his torch from side to side, except for litter and more boxes of rubbish. He wanted to head into the building further, but he started to lose his nerve and stopped where he was, half in and half out of the building. He couldn't decide what to do. His shoulders slumped in defeat at the failed expedition to find the creatures that had been haunting him. He was full of alcohol, but he was starting to see sense. Maybe he should come back tomorrow.

Just as he'd decided to call it a night, a pair of eyes suddenly appeared in the beam of torchlight. A face lifted up from the ground as if it had been asleep, and looked straight at him.

Philip dropped the torch and backed out of the doorway. The door swung shut as a terrible high-pitched screeching sound came from whatever it was that he'd just disturbed. The screeching was accompanied by more noise, seemingly from other creatures. 'Yaahhh!' they screamed. 'Aaarhhh!'

Philip backed away from the building, still holding the knife. He couldn't see much in the darkness, but he could see the door opening. Several different voices screeched and screamed as he turned and ran.

He saw the black creatures standing no higher than the handles of the swinging doors. *Labrador-sized,* he thought once more. But he didn't stay long enough to focus on what they were. He just turned and ran.

He headed back in the direction of the house. Once he was thirty feet or so from the glass building, he quickly turned to see if they were following him. Sure enough, they were. He turned back to see where he was running. There was no time to count them, but he thought there were three of them. Philip's heart pounded hard and his stomach sloshed around with all the bitter he'd drank that evening. He was cold, but he was sweating. As the fear caused his flight from the situation, he was annoyed that he didn't stand his ground. After all, he came looking for them, and now he'd found them, he'd just bolted like before.

As he ran past the pond with the algae covered pedalos, he could finally see the entrance to the underground basement. He ran as fast as he could towards the opening and began to descend the concrete steps, but as he did, the frosty covering caused him to lose his footing and he slipped and rolled to the bottom, dropping the knife as he fell.

Philip hit his head on the dusty floor of the corridor, and although he didn't fall unconscious, he felt woozy, and the pain took hold fast. As he opened his eyes, he could see through blurred vision that the creatures had reached the top of the steps.

They began to scream and screech again, the noise almost deafening.

Philip lay facing the opening with the basement heading to his right, back in the direction of his house.

The screaming creatures came running down the steps, and began to jump on him, hitting him and throwing him around like a ragdoll. He felt pain all over his body; he was pulled up from the ground only to be slammed down hard against the floor. It was like he was being attacked by chimpanzees, only his attacker's voices weren't quite as high-pitched.

Philip couldn't defend himself against the onslaught of violence from these things. He just huddled into a ball to try to survive.

He'd just about given up. He lay there waiting to die, when suddenly, he heard a shout.

'Bah!' the voice shouted.

It was a man's voice. He didn't understand why, but the attack stopped instantly.

Philip looked up, dazed.

The creatures slowly stepped back. As he tried his best to focus in the dark tunnel, he finally saw what they were.

They were human beings; five of them, aged from around six or seven, up to fourteen or so. They now stood upright, whereas before, they seemed to run on all fours. They were dirty, with long, scruffy hair, and dressed, albeit scruffily dressed. They stood back from giving him the beating of his life, panting for breath, and stared at him.

Then, as they slowly stepped away, a man appeared at the top of the concrete steps, dressed in a long coat and carrying a torch.

It was Councillor Fisher.

38

'Bah!' Councillor Fisher said again.

The creatures – the children – stepped away into the darkness of the basement, to Philip's left. Councillor Fisher came slowly down the steps and offered a hand to Philip.

Philip, in a lot of pain and a state of shock, obliged and took his hand.

After helping Philip to his feet, Fisher put an arm around him and helped him along the corridor back to his house.

Neither of them spoke as they travelled the lengthy basement hallway.

Philip groaned and winced with pain, but that was the only noise that either of them made.

A few minutes later, Philip was sat at his kitchen table with a glass of whisky in his shaking hand.

He watched in silence as Councillor Fisher closed the basement door and pushed the armchair back in front of it.

He then sat opposite Philip and poured himself a glass.

Philip didn't really give a thought to the fact that it was Tom's whisky. He felt as though he needed it, even though he'd drank enough that night to put anyone to sleep.

He just sat staring at Councillor Fisher, waiting for him to talk. He knew he didn't have to ask him anything. He knew he didn't have to say anything to the councillor to ask him why these kids were hiding in the amusement park, stealing his food and breaking into his house. He knew he didn't have to ask why they were there, and why they were attacking him. Surely, he was going to finally explain to Philip what'd been going on.

After a few minutes of silence, Philip finished his whisky.

Fisher picked up the bottle and poured him some more, as well as topping up his own glass.

'Do you feel OK?' he finally asked.

'Never better,' Philip said, in a croaky voice. He then began to cough.

Once he'd stopped, Councillor Fisher said, 'That wasn't supposed to happen.'

Philip ached all over. He guessed he was covered in cuts and bruises from the way Fisher's eyes sporadically shifted to different parts of his face. He wanted to look in a mirror to see how bad it was, but first he wanted answers about what the hell was going on.

'I didn't think you'd get so wound up with it all that you'd go in there looking for them. The last tenants, and the tenants before them, thought the place was haunted. I was happy with that. I thought they'd just put up with the strange noises. But neither of them knew about the basement door, you see?'

Philip just listened, while looking him straight in the eye. He didn't want to interrupt the story. He decided he'd let Fisher speak before asking any questions to fill in the blanks.

'Even though I knew you'd found the door, I still didn't expect you to go that far. It's a really creepy place down there. I was hoping it would scare you enough for you to not go through to the park.'

Philip sipped his whisky again.

'All I can say, Philip, is sorry.'

Philip almost laughed at his apology, but everything hurt

so he didn't.

'I really didn't think that would happen.'

It was obvious to Philip that Councillor Fisher was done. So, he thought he'd start to ask some questions, starting with, 'What's your first name?'

Fisher was taken aback. Of all the questions Philip could've asked, he obviously wasn't expecting that one.

'It's Owen. Why?'

'Because I'm sick of this councillor bullshit,' Philip snapped. 'I want to know who they are, why they are there and why it's so important that you have to hold them as prisoners there.'

Fisher shook his head. 'I'm not keeping them prisoners, believe me.'

'Well, what's happening then?'

Fisher took a deep breath, and then a sip of Tom's whisky.

'Owen?' Philip said, addressing him by his given name for the first time.

Owen Fisher began his story.

'They're children, the children of my relatives, the ones that used to own the park. The park has been closed for over five years. And it was only a year or so ago I found out they were there. I, like everyone else in Greysands, thought the place was haunted. I just went along with it. I very rarely went into the park, but one day, I went in and had a good look around. They attacked me. They weren't aware of who I was, they just seemed to panic at me being there. I hit one of them with a lump of wood I'd managed to get my hands on. The fight seemed to stop then. I didn't know what to do. Over time, I got them to trust me.'

'Who knows about this?'

'Nobody.'

'Really?'

'Really. I'm telling you the truth. Everyone thinks the park, this house and the town is being haunted. Gerald thinks they're werewolves. Even Tom didn't know.'

'Tom helped me search the basement the night he died.'

'Really?' Owen asked.

'Yes. I've been thinking that it was the cause if his death.'

Owen shook his head. 'Tom didn't know about the children. But he never believed in ghosts either. I know the basement is scary, but that wouldn't have killed him.'

'No?' Philip said.

'What killed him was poor diet and too much drink. He's not been the same since Betty died. Believe me; it was going to happen sooner or later.'

Philip felt a little relief at what Owen just said. Maybe he wasn't to blame.

'What happened after you discovered the children?' Philip asked.

'Since finding them, I've been working hard to try to help them. I've been trying to teach them how to speak, I've already taught them to dress and use the lavatories in the park. Believe me when I say, that wasn't easy. But they are progressing. They've come a long way.'

'How many of them are there?' Philip asked.

'Five,' Owen replied. 'All of them boys.'

This surprised Philip. 'All boys?'

'Yes. I don't know why, but they're all boys. They range in ages between six and sixteen. I'm guessing of course, but that's what I think.'

'So, let me ask you this, you found them over a year ago, and you've been trying to help them; yes?'

'Yes,' he said. 'I go to see them four times a day, every day. I feed them and make sure they're OK. And I've been trying to communicate with them more and more each time I go.'

'But why haven't you notified the authorities?'

'Because they are my family,' Owen said. 'They will take them away. I can't have that. I have to look after them.'

'But they wouldn't take them away from you altogether. They would get the help they need. They could rebuild their lives for them, instead of them living like feral children.'

'Don't call them that,' Owen said.

'But that's what they are.'

Owen Fisher didn't look happy at the truth about his family, but Philip thought he'd been living in denial for too long. These children needed help.

'They're my family,' Owen said, again.

'They might be your family, but what happened to the rest of your family, the ones that left them there?'

'I don't know. They'd fallen into debt and closed the park eight years ago. The park had been struggling for a long time. It was my uncle that owned it. I didn't really speak to them for the last few years. The park was somewhere that none of the locals ever visited; mainly because my uncle wasn't a very agreeable person. We'd fallen out many years before the park closed. My dad used to try to keep the family together but he was flogging a dead horse.'

'And they just upped sticks and left?'

'Yes,' he said, nodding. 'They were a large family, so I don't even know who the children belonged to. My auntie died several years back, but they had three daughters and four sons. They were all old enough to have children, so it could've been anyone of my cousins, or even a few of them.'

'Why wouldn't they take the children with them?'

'I've gone over this many times in my head and the only thing I could think of is because of their money problems. And maybe they thought someone would go into the amusement park and find them. The park was repossessed by the bank after multiple loans failed to be repaid. So maybe they hoped that someone would've gone in there by now. But nobody has even been to view the place as far as I know.'

'This still doesn't answer my question. Why wouldn't you go to the authorities?'

'I don't know,' he said, holding his head in his hands and looking down at the now-empty whisky glass.

Philip could see guilt in his demeanour. Owen obviously knew he should've acted as soon as he'd found them. But Philip didn't understand why he hadn't.

'I think it was out of shame,' Owen continued. I thought I could help them, and bring them home with me once they trusted me. But it's taken a long time to build up trust, and even now, they won't leave the park with me.'

A sudden thought came to Philip, and the accusation flew from his lips. 'Is this because of your political career?'

Owen Fisher looked offended. He stared at Philip before he finally said, 'I take my political career seriously, but believe me, I wouldn't put it before the wellbeing of mine or anyone else's family.'

Either he was a good actor, or he was telling the truth. Maybe he did think he could help the children. Maybe it had gone on too long for him to go back. Or maybe he was a good liar and there was another reason. Philip didn't know. All he knew was that these kids needed professional help.

'And nobody else knows about this?' Philip asked.

'Just myself,' Owen answered.

'That's it?'

He seemed to think for a moment before saying, 'And Karen and Jack.'

'Jack?'

'The landlord of the pub.'

Philip gave a short laugh. 'So I was right about you four being like the town elders. What about Gerald, does he know?'

Fisher shook his head. 'Honestly, everyone else thinks the park is haunted, including Charlotte. Gerald thinks the place is infested with werewolves. Nobody else knows. Just us three. Four now, including you.'

'I don't believe this,' Philip said.

Fisher nodded as if to agree with Philip that the situation *was* unbelievable.

'Do they ever venture from the park?'

'I told you, they wouldn't come with me. I tried to get them to come…'

'No,' Philip interrupted. 'I'm asking if they ever come out of the park, say, at night?'

He paused as he thought about his answer. 'I believe they have upon a few occasions.'

'You believe they have? Answer the question in a normal way, and not like a politician. They have to have done something in the town for people to keep telling each other to lock their doors.'

'OK. They have wandered into people's houses and stolen things; food mostly.'

'But nobody has ever seen them?'

'Gerald said he saw them once, and a few others have, but it's always at night. Because of the way they walk, hunched over, almost like they're walking on all fours, people didn't identify them as human beings.'

'That's why Gerald thought they were werewolves?'

He nodded.

'So,' Philip said, 'what do we do about this?'

'What can we do?'

'We can tell the police and let them get the help they need.'

'I'm not doing that,' Owen said, getting up from his seat. 'I'm not letting them get dragged away, kicking and screaming. It'll be all over the papers. It'll drag our town and my family through the gutter. To hell with my political career, this place will be a nightmare. There will be press everywhere, people travelling from all over the place to see the freakshow that is Greysands. We can't let that happen.'

Philip sighed. He had to do the right thing. 'We've got to do something.' He then decided to push for more. There had to be more to it for Owen not to go to the police. 'Is there more to this? Is there another reason for not going to the authorities?'

Fisher wiped his forehead and took one more sip of whisky before looking Philip in the eye.

'What is it?'

Fisher took a deep breath. 'They're… malformed.'

'What?'

'They all have, well, most of them have some kind of deformity.'

'In what way?'

'Misshaped limbs mostly.'

'Why does this...' Philip started. Then he realised the problem. 'You think they're the result of inbreeding?'

He nodded.

'Really?'

'Yes. I think my uncle fathered those children with his daughters. And that's what the authorities will think, and that's what the newspapers will think.'

Philip rubbed his face. He'd never felt so tired. He wanted to bring the evening to an end and go to sleep.

'Look, Owen. They are human beings. Even if they were created in this disgusting way, they still deserve a life. They deserve a chance.'

'That's what I'm doing, Philip. I'm trying to help them. They've come a long way since I first found them.'

'But you're not an expert. You've never done this before. This isn't the first-time children have been found living like this. They will be looked after properly and given a second chance at life.'

'I know.'

Philip waited.

'Look, I'm going to go home,' Owen said. 'We'll talk tomorrow, OK?'

Philip nodded.

As Fisher got up to leave, he stopped and turned back. 'I'm really sorry about what happened to you tonight. Will you be OK?'

Philip nodded. 'I'll be fine. Just a few cuts and bruises, that's all.'

'And please, Philip, don't report it. Please let me help them in my own way.'

'We'll talk tomorrow.'

Philip was exhausted, and still a little drunk. He let Owen Fisher out and said goodnight.

His head was spinning with everything that had been going on in his life.

The thoughts of feral children living in his basement was one thing, but he also had to decide what to do over his marriage and his relationship with Charlotte.

What he needed at that moment was a good night's sleep.

He locked the door – which Fisher hadn't told him to do on this occasion – and climbed the stairs. Without even bothering to undress, he fell face first onto his bed.

39

Philip couldn't believe how long he'd slept. It was two-thirty in the afternoon. He felt cloudy-headed and rather sick. He checked himself over after the beating he'd taken the night before and found there was nothing too bad. Just a few cuts and bruises and grazed knees and hips, presumably from when he'd fallen down the concrete steps.

After several cups of tea and a few pieces of toast, he began to feel as though he could function a little. But he had too many things spinning around his head to concentrate on anything. He would've liked to continue with his writing. After all, it had been going very well since moving to Greysands. But more importantly, he had to decide what to do about Owen Fisher and the feral children. He couldn't keep something as important as this to himself. Fisher had asked him, in fact, begged him not to tell anyone. But he couldn't just turn a blind eye to what was going on. They needed help.

He also had to decide on what to do about Charlotte. She'd told him to go and see Lesley and sort things out once and for all. But Charlotte didn't know about Jade Romily and the deception and bribery she'd sprung upon him. The woman and her partner had evidence of him being unfaithful to his wife. Lesley now knew about it, but his faithful readers didn't, and he really hoped to keep it that way.

He was pretty sure his marriage was over, but he was also a little confused after Charlotte pointed out to him that he seemed to try very hard to protect Lesley's feelings when she walked in and saw him with another woman, even though he was completely innocent of any wrongdoing; other than befriending a young and attractive lady. Maybe he had done a little wrong, after all.

He decided to clear his head a little by having a nice hot bath. He lay there trying to decide what he really wanted. The more he thought about it, the more he thought about Charlotte. He wasn't just attracted to her because she was so much younger than him; it was more the fact that she was so sweet and gentle, but still strong and determined. She'd been through a lot, but she was still smiling. This was another reason why he liked her so much. In many ways she was the complete opposite of Lesley.

Lesley was a strong-headed and strong-willed woman, who could win an argument with anyone. Charlotte was much more tender, and other than the telling off she gave him the previous night, he didn't think of her as confrontational at all. Indeed, he thought she was deeply generous at having given him another chance.

He started to feel as though he'd made his decision. But he still had to go and see Lesley. If he had any chance of patching things up with Charlotte, he had to bring his marriage to an end. He did want to see Lesley. It was easy to think of their years together as over when he wasn't in the same room as her. But he had to go and see her to make sure that was how he really felt. He didn't want to do anything rash. He was pretty sure he wanted Charlotte, but he had to be one hundred percent sure.

It was late afternoon by now. Philip wasn't sure what day it was, but he thought it was Friday. He put on his winter coat and went out to the car. The snow was slowly melting, which made it a little easier to drive, but it was still bitterly cold. Once his windscreen had cleared, he set off for home; although he didn't really think of it as home anymore. But it was still the house he owned. He felt confused, almost as confused about that as he did about his failing marriage. He was living in the park house in Greysands, almost like a man on average income. The house was a good-sized one, but since he'd moved there, he hadn't bought any expensive clothes; he hadn't been to any fancy restaurants, and he hadn't had the urge to buy a new car or any other extravagant item. He never thought of himself as a flash millionaire. He'd never showed off with his fortune, and he'd always kept in touch with the people he'd been friends with for years, although he did feel as though he and his friends had lost touch a little.

He enjoyed talking to other successful authors, because they tended to be in the same boat. They were living ordinary lives before suddenly coming into huge amounts of money. So, when other writers invited him to dinner, he accepted. When television presenters and actors or politicians invited him to a dinner party, he politely declined. He didn't want to spend time with a group of people who bragged about their accomplishments. But he was quite happy to sit around a dinner table talking to other authors about writing, and all the things that went with it.

When crime writer Rose Byron asked him to spend the evening with her, he accepted. He and Lesley went to their house and spent a lovely evening with her, her husband and her two children and even Rose's mother. There was no pretentiousness that night. Rose even did the cooking instead of hiring a catering company. He felt as though writers were down to earth, which is where he felt right now, even more so than when he lived at his huge house in Chorley.

He drove for an hour or so. It was six-thirty by the time he'd arrived at his house, or Lesley's house, depending on how the rest of the evening went.

He didn't press his fob to open the electronic gate. He parked up on the road instead, then got out of the Mercedes and walked over to the two metal gates. He then pressed the fob and as they parted, he squeezed through the gap before pressing the fob again to close them behind him.

As he approached the front door, Philip began to wonder if he should've rang the doorbell from the gates. This was still his house, but he hadn't lived there for a few weeks. As he reached the door, he decided to knock.

After waiting for a few minutes, he knocked again. Perhaps Lesley couldn't hear him. The house was large and if she was upstairs or in the kitchen, she might not be able to hear him from where she was.

In the end, he decided to use his key and walk in.

He walked through the long hallway and into the living room. The room looked as it did the last time he saw it. There were two corner sofas in opposite corners of the room, and a glass-topped coffee table that he always felt took up too much space. The large-screened television wasn't switched on, which was unusual. Lesley always had the television on, even if she wasn't watching it. She used to say that their house was eerily quiet, so left the television on whether she was watching it or not.

'Lesley!' he shouted.

There was no answer.

He left the living room and wandered through to the kitchen. This was the room where Philip liked to spend his time, if he wasn't in his office, that was. The large room had jet-black cupboards with marbled worktops. The kitchen island had a small flat screen television on top, where he used to catch up with the news or the occasional football match. He had followed football religiously when he was younger, but as his writing career progressed, he kept missing matches, getting caught up in his stories and forgetting about them. Now if he ever found the time to watch a match, he never seemed to know who any of the players were. Unless he'd seen them on the news for behaving badly in public or having affairs or getting caught drinking and driving.

As he was about to leave the empty kitchen, he jumped when Lesley walked in. She was in her dressing gown and looked a little flustered to see him there.

'What are you doing here?' she said.

'I wanted to talk,' Philip said.

'You can't just turn up like this, Philip. I told you to stay away until I contacted you. In fact, the last thing I told you was that I wanted a divorce.'

It's my house and I'll turn up whenever I bloody well feel like it, he thought, but didn't say the words aloud.

'Look, Lesley, I want to talk.'

'Well I don't want to talk to you. I'm going out soon and I'm getting ready.'

Philip looked at his watch. 'It's only six-thirty. Surely you have time?'

'Sandra just called. Mick has gone out and she's bored. I'm going to nip round for a chat and a bit of supper.'

'Well, can we talk first,' he said, pulling out a chair to the kitchen island.

'You've got a nerve,' she said.

'What do you mean?'

She put her hands on her hips and looked even more annoyed. 'First you cheat on me, risking everything we've worked hard for…'

Everything I've worked hard for.

'Then I walk in to find you've been at it with that tart …'

Calling Charlotte a tart infuriated him. He could feel his anger growing.

'… and then you turn up unannounced and expect me to put my evening plans on hold so we can talk about everything you've done to ruin our marriage.'

'Look, first of all, Charlotte isn't a tart, and secondly, there is nothing going on between us.'

'You were in your dressing gown when Daniel came to see you!' she shouted.

'I'd fallen down the stairs the night before. Didn't you see the bruise on my face? I was lay at the bottom of the stairs all night. Charlotte called to say hello and when I told her what had happened and how crappy I felt, she ran me a bath to help me feel better.'

Lesley stood shaking her head, jaw twitching from side to side. She obviously didn't believe that nothing was going on with him and Charlotte. Although Philip felt as though there was a blossoming relationship, he was technically telling the truth because he hadn't even kissed Charlotte yet; not that he hadn't thought about it.

'Do you know what this would do to your career as a writer, if it got out to your followers about the way you've been behaving? It could ruin you. You'd never sell a book again.'

He didn't quite believe that, but he did agree with her that keeping the Jade Romily situation from the press was the best thing to do.

'How do we know that woman isn't going to leak the video to the press?'

'We don't. But she hasn't so far, so maybe she won't.'

Lesley shook her head. 'Any day now she could ruin our lives even more than she already has. Do you know how humiliating it would be to have the whole world see that video? See what you did? I don't think I could show my face in public again.'

'I know ...'

He suddenly stopped talking because he heard a noise above his head. He looked at the ceiling and listened for any more noises. The single dull thud was the only noise he heard, but it was enough to change the temperature of the room.

He looked at Lesley. Her face reddened as she pulled an expression of exaggerated puzzlement.

In that moment, as he argued with his wife, or soon to be ex-wife, that noise upstairs brought everything crashing into place. It wasn't just the noise; it was the actions of a woman who'd just been found out. A woman who held all the cards close to her chest. A woman who was about to have a very strong wind blow those cards from her grasp and onto the floor.

Philip shook his head slowly as he looked at her with utter contempt. This woman who he'd been married to for a quarter of a century, and helped him through his career and his life, now looked completely different to him.

He was disgusted at the person he saw in front of him. He couldn't believe she'd done this. He couldn't believe that she'd be so deceitful and so hypocritical.

He jumped off the chair and ran past her.

'Philip!' she shouted, but he ignored her and ran up the stairs as fast as he could, then along the landing to the master bedroom, the room that had been their marital bedroom. He burst the door open to find nobody in there.

But he still wasn't happy. Something made that noise, and it definitely wasn't a group of feral children. Someone was in there.

The bed wasn't as neatly made as it normally was, but it also didn't look messy and slept in.

Even though it felt like an obvious scene from many of the films he'd seen over the years, he knew he had to look in the wardrobe.

He slid the doors to one side. Nothing.

He moved to the other side and slid that door open.

Inside the wardrobe, looking back at him, was a man he knew very well.

40

Daniel stood there in Philip's wardrobe looking back at him. His agent, his friend, his advisor, his partner throughout his career. This man had now betrayed him. Daniel's huge frame filled the space, the most pitiful expression Philip had ever seen on his face.

Although Daniel looked as though he'd never lost a fight in his life, he also gave the impression that he'd never have needed to get into a fight. If he looked angry, you'd back away. But Philip thought of him as a gentle giant. He could be tough and ruthless when dealing with people with regards to Philip's literary career, but he'd never thought of him as a violent man. But right now, at that moment, Philip was about to find out just how tough he was.

Daniel remained in the closet, dressed in his shirt and trousers, but his clothes were untidy, which was something Philip had never seen before. His shirt wasn't tucked in properly and he wasn't wearing his usual tie or even a pair of shoes.

There was no doubt in Philip's mind what was happening. He clenched his fist and swung a punch at Daniel. He was very aware that it had to be a good one. A man Daniel's size wasn't going to fall easily. Even though he didn't fancy his chances in a fight against this man, he had no doubts that throwing a punch at him was the only thing to do at that very moment. Daniel had done something you should never do to a friend, and he needed to know how angry Philip felt at his betrayal.

The punch landed hard on Daniel's left cheek, making a loud slapping sound, like a sound effect in a Kung Fu movie.

Daniel's head fell to the side. He didn't fall down but he stumbled and struggled to get his balance.

Before Philip could swing a second punch his way, a sudden pain filled his head and he fell forward onto the thick bedroom carpet. He didn't know what had happened, but the pain spread and he drifted off into unconsciousness.

41

Philip couldn't open his eyes because of the pounding in his head. Every beat of his heart sent a dull ache through his skull as he lay face down on the carpet. He could hear voices; the voices of his wife, Lesley, and his friend and agent, Daniel. They were muffled, as if they were in the distance. But rather than try to open his eyes, he kept them firmly shut and stayed still.

'We can't do that,' Daniel said. 'Are you crazy?'

'Well, what do you suggest?' Lesley shouted at him.

'This is all getting out of hand,' Daniel said, sounding stressed. His voice seemed to travel around the room as if he was pacing around.

'We have to kill him,' Lesley said. 'We can make it look like self-defence.'

Philip couldn't believe that the woman he'd been married to for twenty-five years now wanted him dead. Was Daniel really worth it? No, he wasn't, Philip thought. There had to be more to it than that.

He tried to work out what position he was in. His head pounded from the blow that had been thrust upon him by his ever-loving wife as he tried to teach Daniel that friendship wasn't something he took lightly. Daniel had obviously been having an affair with Lesley. But was that really enough to kill for?

Philip wondered if it was his fortune. That was it. It must

be. Daniel must've swooped in after Philip's misdemeanour and swept Lesley off her feet. But did he love her? Or was Daniel just after the money? Daniel had squandered away most of his earnings from years of hard work when he developed an online gambling habit. He'd previously confided in Philip that he would've been a millionaire by now, based on his fifteen percent shares in all the authors on his portfolio. But instead of that, he lived in the two-bedroom terraced house his parents left him in their will.

As he lay face down on the carpet in what was once his master bedroom, Philip wondered if Lesley had fallen for Daniel's charms and not realised he was just after her for her money. Not even her money; although Philip knew that he'd need a very good lawyer to stop her taking at least fifty percent. If they'd got married when he was a millionaire, he could've looked into a prenuptial agreement. But when they got married, although they were comfortable, they didn't have the fortune they had today.

He felt numb as he lay still, listening to Lesley and Daniel panic. He tried to move his arms just a little, wanting to check he wasn't tied up. He had to be very slight with his movements so as to not give away to them that he was now conscious.

The last few weeks flashed through his mind. He'd been through so much; Jade Romily, moving to Greysands, being haunted by the feral children, making friends with Tom, only to lose him. And now, he was in his own home being held hostage by his wife and his agent.

He now knew that Lesley wanted him dead. But although all these things were going through his mind, the biggest thought in his head was the fact that he wanted to get back to Charlotte;

even more so now he knew the truth about Lesley and Daniel.

He knew his marriage was over. But at that moment, he didn't care, and he didn't care what Lesley and Daniel had been up to, even in his bed. He didn't even care about his fortune or his career. He was falling in love with Charlotte, and he was falling in love with Greysands. He wanted this situation to be over so he could go back to what he now thought of as home.

He didn't think he was tied up. He could only move his hands a little but realised that, although they were pointing downwards, they were at his sides and too far apart to be tied. He was trying so hard to stay still that his body was numb all over.

He lay on his front, his head to the left. Lesley and Daniel's voices were to his right, so he decided to open his eyes.

He had a blurry sideways view of the open wardrobe. A large object was on the floor in front of him, but he couldn't focus well enough to tell what it was. As he gave up and stopped trying to bring the object into focus, he realised what it was. It was a metal saucepan, and not one of the smaller ones, he thought. It was now obvious to him that Lesley had grabbed it from the kitchen before making her way upstairs and used it to knock him out. His head almost began to hurt more just at the realisation of what had hit him.

'I'll go and get a knife,' Lesley said.

This sentence made his stomach flip.

'We can't do that,' Daniel said, hissing through his teeth.

Nobody spoke after that, so Philip presumed she'd left the room.

He wondered if now was a good time to act. He still felt numb, but hoped the fear of whatever Lesley was about to do would kick-start the adrenaline so he could fight back or defend himself somehow.

He waited to give her a chance to get far enough down the stairs. Then, as his heart rate quickened, he flipped himself over and jumped up from the floor.

As he turned, he saw Daniel's huge frame perched on the edge of *his* bed. His eyes widened. Even though Daniel was a great big bear of a man, he looked scared as he paused, obviously wondering what to do.

Philip lunged at him and grabbed by the front of his shirt. He put all his strength into pulling him forward and throwing him to the floor.

As Daniel fell backwards, Philip swung a punch at him. He still felt woozy, sick and faint from the blow to the head, and although he didn't know how long he was out for, it was clearly long enough to make him feel nauseous. But he still found the fight inside him to act before he was murdered in his own house.

The punch hit Daniel on his temple, sending him flying backwards to the floor.

Philip didn't feel as though he'd hit him as hard as the first time, but it was good enough to knock him over.

Daniel quickly sat back up, holding a hand out to try and stop any further blows from hitting him.

Philip swung a fist once more, catching him across the jaw.

He started to think that Daniel wasn't even trying to fight back, almost as though his guilt at sleeping with Philip's wife was stopping him from doing so. But Philip didn't want to take anything for granted. If a man Daniel's size decided to fight back, he knew he wouldn't stand a chance. So, he grabbed him by the shirt with his left hand and sent his right fist thrusting towards him again.

The punch hit hard this time. Daniel's expression changed from stern to a dizzying look as if this one had really hurt him, making Philip think that the first two hadn't.

Daniel's limp body hit the floor and although he didn't stay still, he looked as though the fight was over. He lay there writhing as he rolled over slowly, trying to stand, but he couldn't.

Daniel was out of action enough for Philip to leave him and look for Lesley.

He turned and walked to the bedroom door, picking up the discarded saucepan. It wasn't an ideal weapon, but it might help him against an attack from a mad woman waving a kitchen knife. No doubt she'd have gone for the largest from the rack, the ones they rarely used when preparing meals.

He poked his head through the doorway and quickly jumped backwards, just in case she was waiting for him. She wasn't there, but she must've heard the noise from the beating he'd just given Daniel; albeit a polite beating, considering what he'd done.

Philip made his way along the landing to the banister that overlooked most of the hallway below. He still couldn't see her. He wondered if she was still in the kitchen so he listened, but couldn't hear anything. So he started heading down the stairs, slowly, one step at a time.

The kitchen came into view and although he couldn't see all of the room, what he could see made his heart beat faster. The wooden knife rack that housed six knives had an empty slot; the slot at the top where the ten-inch knife would usually reside.

He wondered what he should do. He'd been assaulted, so

he could phone the police. But did he want everyone to find out what had happened, and that his wife had been cheating on him? He thought for a moment. His wife was planning to kill him and was hiding somewhere in the house with a knife, so yes, phoning the police would be the right thing to do. But first he had to get to a phone.

As he walked through the doorway to the kitchen, he quickly scanned the room looking for Lesley. He couldn't see her anywhere in the room. He walked around the kitchen island, checking underneath as he did; nothing. Where had she gone?

He walked over to the counter where the knives were, not to get a knife, but to go to the phone that sat next to the rack. As he got there a found the cradle empty. He wondered if Lesley had the phone with her, or if she'd just left it somewhere in the house as usual. For the first time in his life, he wished he had a mobile phone.

He put the saucepan down and took out the long, heavy knife sharpener from the kitchen drawer. He didn't want to carry a knife, even though he knew Lesley had one, but he had to have something to defend himself with. He thought the sharpener would be a good enough weapon to disarm her. Even though he was the one being attacked, he didn't want to kill her, for his own sake more than hers. He'd written many stories about murder, but he didn't want to have one on his conscience for the rest of his life, even if he didn't get sent to prison for it.

The air in the room was still. All he could hear was the humming noise of the fridge-freezer; apart from that there wasn't a sound. He walked back through the kitchen doorway and along the hallway into the living room. He looked around the room, checking all four corners as he held the knife sharpener in front of him, ready to swing.

The living room – the room he hardly ever spent any time in – was the biggest room in the house, except for the annex that housed the swimming pool.

He walked around the sofas, making sure she wasn't hiding behind them.

After doing a circuit of the room, he was just about to walk through the doorway when he heard a noise above his head. The room above the living room was his office. It sounded like something had fallen; maybe a book from one of the many shelves, or perhaps an ornament, or maybe his Booker Prize.

He ran upstairs and headed towards the office, then stopped as he reached the doorway, just in case Lesley was waiting inside the door. He couldn't see her so he pushed the door further open, thinking she might be hiding behind it. It opened all the way; she wasn't there.

He saw the cause of the bang lying on the floor. It was a book. He walked over and picked it up. It was his signed copy of *The Outsider* by Stephen King. This was an item he treasured. He'd never met Stephen King but he'd spoken to him on the phone a few times and they'd exchanged signed copies of their latest novels. Philip sent him a copy of *The Bridge*, a novel that was his favourite up to that point, and he was even more happy with it once Stephen King had phoned him a second time to say how much he'd loved it. Luckily, Philip had finished reading *The Outsider* that day. He would've been embarrassed at having a conversation about his own novel if he hadn't have read King's. But luckily it all worked out.

He closed the book, folding the bent pages back into place,

and put it back on the shelf.

No sooner had he done this, when he turned to see Lesley in the doorway, running at him with her hand held high, the hand that held the ten-inch knife. She brought the knife down and without thinking, he brought the sharpener in front of him, swinging it in a back-handed motion. It caught her on the wrist and she shouted with pain, but she held onto the knife and brought it back for a second try.

Although Philip heard her say to Daniel that she wanted to kill him, he didn't fully believe that she was capable. But now, in his office, the room where all the magic happened, he was certain she was serious about putting an end to his life.

He jumped backwards from the knife as it cut the air just in front of his chest. He managed to hit her hand again with the sharpener, but she still didn't drop the knife.

He could see the rage on her face. It was a look he'd never seen before. Obviously, he'd seen her angry, but the expression on her face now was pure rage. She looked almost evil, like a character from one of his novels.

She thrust the hand with the knife at him again.

His right hand held the sharpener, but he instinctively put his left arm up to block the blow. Even though he was still wearing his winter coat, the knife went through the material and tore his flesh.

He screamed with pain, then lifted the sharpener above his head and brought it down hard across her face. It was at that point he knew that he'd previously just been trying to hold her off. Maybe because she was his wife, or maybe because he was fighting with a woman; he didn't know. But he now knew, after feeling the cold steel of the knife cut his arm, that he had to become more ruthless if he was going to survive this battle. He had to put her out of action.

The metal of the sharpener made a loud crack as it hit her face. But it didn't stop her.

She lunged at him again.

Philip grabbed her wrist, dropping the sharpener as he did.

Engulfed by rage, she pushed him backwards into the bookshelf, sending books falling to the ground.

She growled at him, just like the feral children had. Only he now knew the children were defending their territory. Lesley wanted him dead and he knew that nothing less than dead would suffice.

He pushed her away, sending her into the desk opposite the bookshelf, her dressing gown flailing open. But no sooner had he done this, when she adjusted herself and swung the knife back in his direction, cutting his coat across the chest. He wasn't sure if it'd gone through to his body, but he certainly felt the pressure of the blow.

She went at him again, and they tussled and fought. He was aware of the knife as he grabbed her wrist once more, but he was also aware of how strong she was. She visited the gym on a regular basis, but it was the rage that was giving her the strength to fight so hard.

As he put all his efforts into pushing her and the knife away from him, there was a sudden pain on the right side of his face, sending him flying backwards against the desk and onto the floor.

Philip felt as though his face was on fire and his headache returned.

As he opened his eyes, he saw Daniel standing over him,

looking more menacing than before. Obviously, the guilt of stealing his wife had worn off, Philip thought.

Daniel just stood there, staring at him.

Lesley stood at his side, fastening her dressing gown and breathing heavily from the fight.

Philip didn't know what would happen now. It all still seemed extreme behaviour to him. But with Daniel towering over him and Lesley still holding the knife as if it was glued to her hand, he didn't see a way out of the situation.

'Why?' he asked. 'Why are you doing this?'

Neither of them answered.

'You can have each other,' Philip shouted. 'I don't give a shit. But why do I have to die? I cheated first remember. You'll get your divorce settlement, so why do you have to kill me?'

This question seemed to cause a change in their demeanour. They both looked a little puzzled. Philip didn't understand why.

Lesley and Daniel looked at each other. They seemed to have a conversation without actually speaking. They widened their eyes and raised their eyebrows.

Philip couldn't help but feel as though he was missing something. He'd cheated on his wife, moved away, and come back to find her having an affair with Daniel. This was a horrible situation, but was it really worth killing for?

Then it hit him, like a bolt of electricity flying through his body. It wasn't just the two of them having an affair. It was the whole situation. It all made sense – Jade Romily, Daniel's gambling problem, their relationship – it suddenly all made sense.

'I don't believe it,' Philip said. 'It was you two all along.'

He dragged himself up from the floor.

'It isn't just that you two have been at it behind my back now, it's been going on the whole time.'

Their expressions became guilty, and their shoulders dropped. Lesley's jaw continued to twitch.

'All the times you were out of the house,' he said, addressing Lesley, 'and the many times I would come home and find you here,' he continued, pointing to Daniel. 'You've been having an affair the whole time, and you orchestrated the indiscretion with Jade Romily, didn't you? That's why I have to die. That's how she knew how much money was in my account.'

'No. That's not what happened,' Lesley said.

Philip didn't have to argue. Daniel's reaction said it all as he turned to her and said, 'Come on, Lesley. He knows. There's no point denying it. We've been found out.'

Lesley looked deeply annoyed with Daniel, but she didn't speak.

'So that's it,' Philip said. 'You hired an escort to get me drunk and seduce me, you then tried to bribe me, and when I didn't play ball and your plan failed, you just settle for the divorce settlement?'

'That was plan B, yes,' Lesley snapped. 'We thought you'd be a coward and keep sending payments to keep her quiet. But the plan still worked to a point because you would have to pay me more, because of you being unfaithful.'

Philip shook his head. 'How long has this been going on?'

Daniel answered, 'Only a year or so.'

'A *year?*' Philip shouted.

He couldn't believe what he'd heard; he couldn't believe any of it. He didn't know how to bring it to an end. All he knew was that he wanted to get out of the house and as far away from them as possible.

'This ends now,' he said. He then started to walk past them, but Lesley moved quickly to stand in his way.

'Let me pass,' Philip said, quietly but sternly as he sporadically looked at each of them straight in the eye.

'We can't do that,' Lesley said, still holding the ten-inch kitchen knife.

Philip wasn't sure what was going to happen.

Daniel seemed to accept defeat. He turned to Lesley and said, 'Look, it's over.'

Lesley's eyes widened. 'It's not over yet.'

'Lesley,' Daniel said. 'It *is* over. He knows. There's no going back now.'

She slowly shook her head from side to side. 'There's no way I'm going to prison.'

'Well maybe we can strike up a deal,' Daniel said.

Typical Daniel, Philip thought. Trying to buy his way out of trouble. Philip knew there was nothing they could offer him. Apart from the knife pointing towards him, the cards were stacked in his favour.

'I can't go to prison,' she said, once more.

'Look,' Philip said, 'this whole situation is ridiculous. I'm going, and I'm going now. Kill me if you want, but it'll only make things worse for you.'

With that, Daniel stood aside. 'Go, Philip. I never meant for it to go this far. Go. Phone the police. Do whatever you have to do.'

Philip looked at Lesley one last time as he walked away. She stood there, still in her dressing gown, still holding the knife, and still wearing an expression of pure hatred. He couldn't help but think what he'd done to deserve this from her. Why couldn't she settle for just telling him she didn't love him anymore, and keeping her relationship with Daniel a secret until the divorce was final? She'd still have left the marriage with a decent amount of money from the settlement. Why did she have to come up with this ridiculous charade? Or was Daniel the brains behind it all? And how much did he actually owe from his gambling debts? Philip just wanted to get away from them both, call the police and let his solicitors deal with it all. Above all he wanted to get back to Charlotte.

As he walked past them, Lesley went to lunge again, but Daniel stopped her and held her back.

Philip then left the room and made his way down the stairs, pulling his sleeve back as he walked, to reveal a deep cut to his forearm. The gash was about four inches long, and it was bleeding enough to soak his sleeve. He didn't mind blood spots hitting the carpet. After all, any blood traces might be useful if Daniel and Lesley denied what had happened. To be sure, before rolling his sleeve back down, he held his arm low and let some of the blood drip to the floor. He knew from his time in the police force and from the research he'd done for his novels that it was hard to remove all traces of blood, even with bleach.

He wondered when he'd have to come to the house again. He knew it would be just to collect his belongings. Even once they were divorced, he couldn't see himself wanting to live here again. He couldn't see himself living anywhere but Greysands ever again.

Philip headed along the hallway to the front door. As he grabbed the handle, a loud screaming sound, almost a growl, came from his left and he turned to see Lesley running at him with the knife held high.

He held his arm up again and as before, he felt the knife dig into his flesh. He shouted with pain and kicked a foot out at her. The sole of his shoe hit her left thigh, sending her backwards as her leg buckled. She stumbled, but managed to stay on her feet.

Philip was furious. He'd tried his best upstairs not to get into a fight, and had just tried to subdue her. But that wasn't going to work now. Lesley was out of control.

He went to grab the knife, as he had upstairs, but she reacted quickly and pulled it away, the blade slicing across the base of his fingers.

He kicked out again, this time thrusting at her knee, and she fell backwards onto the floor, landing in a sitting position, and still waving the knife towards him.

He tried to kick her hand as she waved the knife from side to side, but he couldn't stop her.

She stopped waving the knife and pointed it at Philip, still snarling like a madwoman, then got to her feet and held him at bay with her spiteful grimace and ten-inch blade.

Philip was closer to the door, but he couldn't turn his back on her. The woman he'd once loved and who'd once loved him seemed determined to bring his life to an end. He couldn't let her win. He knew that if she killed him, she would be able to turn the story around and let him go to his grave with everyone thinking of him as a cold-hearted monster who'd tried to kill his own wife. That wasn't going to happen.

He jumped backwards as Lesley cut the air in front of him once more, his back hitting the solid wood of the front door.

She took a step towards him and tried to stick the knife

straight into his stomach.

He stepped aside and threw a punch at her arm. It landed, but not hard enough to stop her.

She brought the knife above her head, as she had before. This time she was only inches from him, so instead of going for the knife, he threw a right hook, catching her on her left cheek.

Her expression of anger dispersed immediately as she fell to the floor and lay still on her back.

Philip took a moment to catch his breath. He waited for her to move, but she didn't.

She lay there, her dressing gown slightly open, revealing her naked body, her arms out to the sides. The knife was still in her hand, but her grip on it had loosened.

Philip watched for a moment, until he saw her chest rise and fall. She was breathing, but not as heavily as he was. He knew he'd hit her hard, but he didn't want to kill her.

Panic suddenly crept in as he wondered if he'd done her harm, and what would happen to him if she died.

He stepped over her and crouched at her side. Her breathing stopped. He pressed two fingers onto her neck, feeling for a pulse. As he did so, her eyes shot open and she jumped up, trying to stab him once more. He fell backwards.

Lesley was up within a second and lunged at him again.

He grabbed her wrist with both hands as she fell on top of him with all her weight. He pushed the knife away from him as she landed.

Suddenly she froze. Her eyes widened, and her mouth fell open. She didn't breathe as she stared into his eyes, only inches away from him. She then gave a cough, but still didn't breathe in.

Philip put all his strength into pushing her off him and rolling her away.

He then saw that the partially open dressing gown wasn't white any longer. A dark red area had formed around the stomach area, where the knife was sticking out of the gap in the gown.

She landed on her back and gazed up at him. She then began to take deep croaky breaths as if she'd been under water. She writhed from side to side as she held onto the knife that Philip could see was embedded deep inside her.

He pulled the dressing gown apart, but immediately wished he hadn't. The knife was in almost up to the wooden handle. Dark puddles formed and spilled over her white flesh, running down to the hard wood floor.

He knew she didn't stand a chance of surviving, but he had to try. He started to get up, but Lesley grabbed his arm tightly. It was the arm she'd previously cut and it hurt when she grabbed it, but he ignored the pain as he watched his wife struggle for breath.

She coughed and spluttered but still kept her eyes on him, and Philip knew this was an image that would stay with him forever.

Her skin faded, and her grip on his arm weakened. Her hand then fell to the floor as her eyes rolled backwards.

She didn't move again.

42

Philip stood up.

He couldn't believe what had just happened. His wife was lying on the floor of their hallway, dead, with a knife still stuck in her stomach.

Would he be charged with murder? Surely not; he was defending himself, after all. He had to think what to do. It momentarily crossed his mind to hide the body, but he knew that wouldn't work. It didn't work for any of the characters in his books and it wouldn't work for him. He knew he had to phone the police, and fast. If he told the truth he'd be fine.

The only problem was, he didn't know where Lesley had hidden the phones.

He ran upstairs as quickly as he could, then went along the landing and headed for his office. As he reached the doorway, he saw another scene of horror.

Daniel was sat up on the floor, leaning against the book-shelves. He was upright, but his head was slumped to one side. There was blood soaking the front of his shirt, so much so that Philip couldn't see the entry wound. His mobile phone was on the floor next to him. Philip wondered if he'd phoned the police. He picked up the phone – not needing to check Daniel's pulse as he was obviously dead – and pressed the screen several times to try and figure out how to make the call. He wasn't familiar with mobile phones, but he knew that previous calls appeared on the screen when you did this. He pressed the green phone symbol. The last call he'd made was to Lesley, so Philip dialled nine nine nine.

43

The next several hours were a blur. Philip told the full story to the police officers that were the first to arrive at the scene, then the detectives, then the detectives again at the station as he sat dressed in a paper suit. He didn't think they believed his story. He found the whole ordeal difficult to focus on. Although he wanted to get back to Greysands, and back to Charlotte, the thing he wanted more than anything was sleep.

He didn't feel as though he was defending his innocence very well, but he just couldn't concentrate. Repeatedly telling the story was like doing a final edit on one of his novels. He just wanted it over with so he could move on. But they just kept asking the same questions, again and again.

His solicitor tried to get him released on bail, but it wasn't to be. After the detectives heard his final rendition of the story – which he told word for word the same as the previous seven times – they put him into a cell where he could finally close his eyes.

He guessed it was one or two in the morning by now. It wasn't unusual for him to be awake at that hour, but he was done in. As soon as his head hit the uncomfortably flat pillow, he drifted off to sleep.

The cell door opened and Detective Wallace, who'd interviewed Philip before he'd slept, walked inside. He was a stocky man, medium height, in his early thirties. He was clean shaven and had short dark hair.

'Mr Lloyd,' he said.

Philip sat up on the bed. He felt really groggy, and he immediately noticed the pain in his arm where the knife had twice cut him. The paramedics had bandaged it up, once they realised that Lesley and Daniel were beyond help. Philip wasn't really aware of the pain during the interviews, but now it was throbbing.

He finally managed to open his eyes properly and focus on the man standing in front of him.

'Mr Lloyd, there's been a development. We need to get you back to the interview room.'

'What is it?'

'You'll see. Come on. There's a cup of tea waiting for you.'

As he sat down, Philip realised that his solicitor wasn't there. He waited until the detective, who was now sitting next to a different detective than before, had finished doing the statement for the tape before saying, 'Where's my solicitor?'

'You don't need one,' Detective Wallace said. 'You're free to go.'

Suddenly, Philip felt very awake. 'Really?'

Wallace nodded.

'Well, why are we in here then?'

Wallace picked up two thin plastic gloves off the desk and put them on. Also on the desk was a mobile phone in a plastic resealable bag. Once the detective had the gloves on, he started to remove the phone from the bag.

'For the recording,' he said, 'I'm showing Mr Lloyd the mobile phone, belonging to Daniel Johnson who was found at the scene. I'm about to play him the video that was found on it.'

Philip was confused. Daniel couldn't have filmed the scuffle that resulted in Lesley falling onto the knife. Surely he would have still been in the same place in the office where she'd stabbed him?

Wallace started the video, holding the phone in both hands with the screen facing towards Philip.

The footage was shaky as the camera shot all around Philip's office until finally it rested on Daniel, in his position on the floor. Daniel then held the camera reasonably still and aimed it at his own face.

He spoke quietly to the camera as he took quick, short breaths.

'She's gone mad ... It's still going on ... Here's what happened. I'm telling you because it's gone too far, and she's lost her mind.'

He winced with pain, his voice tired and groggy, as the sweat poured from his forehead.

'Lesley and I have been having an affair for over a year. I have financial problems, and she came up with the plan of extorting money from Philip. We hired an escort to seduce him and film it ... He refused to pay so ... so we decided just to push for the divorce. He came home and caught us here and then ... then it got out of hand. She tried stabbing him, I stopped her, but as Philip left the room to leave, she stabbed me. She's now gone looking for him ...'

As he said that line, Philip could hear her scream in the background, possibly from when Lesley lunged at him with the knife.

Sweat poured down his face. He winced as he fought for breath.

'Whatever happens ... Philip is innocent. Lesley is trying to kill him so she ... she can turn it around and blame him ... self-defence ...' He grew weaker as the video continued. The phone slipped a little as he struggled to hold on to it. He wasn't in the shot any more.

'Philip isn't to blame ... he didn't ...' After a few seconds of wheezing sounds from Daniel, the phone hit the floor.

Wallace turned the phone off and returned it to the bag.

'After a few minutes, you come in and turn the phone off. Presumably to phone for us.'

Philip nodded. 'Yes. I don't have a mobile phone so it took a minute for me to figure it out.'

Detective Wallace nodded and gave a slight smile.

The other detective then spoke for the first time. 'Is everything he said true?'

'It is,' Philip said.

He couldn't believe that the person he now hated, the person who had been lying to him all this time and seeing his wife behind his back, had suddenly had an attack of conscience. He wondered why Daniel didn't phone the police himself. But he then realised that if Lesley had got the better of Philip and killed him, if Daniel survived, he could've gone along with Lesley's lie of self-defence to keep himself in the clear.

He could never forgive Daniel for what he did, but he was glad he made the video before he died. Now Philip could go home. Not his home in Chorley, but his home in Greysands.

The police took him back to the house to get changed and get his car back.

Scenes of crime officers were still there, but they let him get some clothes, so he could drive back to Greysands. They stayed with him as he searched for something to wear then got dressed. Philip knew he'd have a lot to organise, but for now, he just wanted to get as far away from this house as possible. And that's what he did.

44

It was seven in the morning by the time Philip arrived at what he now thought of as his home. The snow had all but disappeared, and although the sun wasn't up yet, the town felt much brighter to him. As he drove along the sea-front, heading towards his house, he couldn't help but smile.

He felt as though he'd been conditioned into needing a huge bank balance and everything that came with being rich, in order to be happy. But now, he really didn't care about his old house being left empty. There was a top-quality security system in place that had police response, but even so, he still really didn't care.

He wanted to put the house up for sale as soon as possible, and maybe look at buying the park house. There would also be other things to sort out, like funerals for one. Even though he and Lesley weren't together, and even though she'd tried to kill him, he'd still have to arrange her funeral. But at that moment, he didn't want to think about that; he just wanted to get home.

He was still smiling as he parked up on his drive and got out of the car.

He looked around at the ocean as the waves crashed onto the shore. The lighthouse stood at the top of the hill, looking as beautiful as ever.

He knew he would continue to write. Once the writing bug gets hold of you it's impossible to break free, no matter what's going on in your life. But he thought that maybe he would take a step back and slow things down a little. He didn't have an agent anymore, but he thought he could speak to his publisher about continuing to work without one and just go at his own pace. Money wasn't an issue. But no doubt the story of his wife and agent trying to extort money from him and then trying to kill him would overshadow his writing career for a while; or maybe enhance it. Hadn't someone once said there was no such thing as bad publicity? But for now, he was just glad to be home. He very badly wanted to see Charlotte, but at this time in the morning, she'd probably still be asleep, especially as she had most likely been working in the pub the previous evening.

He walked into his house, locked the door behind him, and saw the chair that was still in front of the basement door.

That was a situation that needed dealing with as soon as possible. But his head was still spinning. He went upstairs and ran a bath. He removed his clothes and the bandages. He knew the water would sting the cuts on his arms, but he didn't care. He needed to wash the previous day's events away. Having a bath felt like a new start for him. He fell asleep in the hot soapy water as tiredness got the better of him. When he woke, he climbed out of the bath, got into bed and fell into a deep sleep.

45

It was late morning when Philip woke up. After getting dressed and having some toast, he opened the curtains to let the winter sun brighten up the living room. He sat at his desk. He had no intentions of doing any writing just yet, but he wanted to enjoy the view and allow his thoughts to go where they needed to. He still didn't want to get himself stressed about the events of the next couple of months, be it funerals or selling his house, or anything else he had to do. He just wanted to relax and enjoy the day.

As he leaned forward, he saw a police car to his left. He hoped it was nothing to do with him and what had happened the day before.

He got up from his seat and leaned into the bay window to get a better view. When he did, he could see more police cars – three in total. He ran to his hallway and put his winter coat on – even though there was a rip in the sleeve – and left the house.

As he reached the dirt track that led to the amusement park, he saw more police cars, two police vans and two ambulances.

He walked along the track towards the park. At the bottom, there were a dozen or so police officers all standing at the open metal gate that reached across the track.

When a police officer saw him, he quickly came over. 'Sir, you can't come down here,' he said, holding his hand up.

'What's happened?' Philip asked. 'I live in the house you see.'

'It's a police matter, sir. I can't say any more than that.'

'Is it the children?'

The officer suddenly stopped and looked at him. 'You know about the children living here?'

'Yes; well, sort of. I only found out yesterday.' He wasn't sure if it was yesterday or the day before. He was still all over the place with times and events.

'Philip,' he heard someone shout.

When he looked over the officer's shoulder, he saw Owen Fisher coming towards him, dressed in a suit as usual. Only there was something different about him. His face wore an expression Philip had never seen before. As he got closer, Philip realised what it was; Fisher had been crying.

'It's OK, officer; he's with me,' he said. He then put an arm around Philip and walked him into the park.

'What's going on?'

'I did what you said. I phoned the authorities. I told them everything. I told them I'd been trying to look after them, and that I'd kept it a secret.'

'What have they done?'

'They've just got them into the police vans. I've had to show them around the park, including the tunnel, but I didn't take them into your house.'

'Why are you so upset?' Philip asked.

They stopped as Fisher turned to face him.

'It was horrible,' Fisher said, biting his lip, trying not to cry. 'I've never seen them so scared.'

'Were the police aggressive with them?'

'Not really. I mean, they had to be tough about it to get them into the vans. It's just that ... they weren't happy, and they're especially not happy at being dragged away like that. They don't understand.'

For the first time since Philip met Owen Fisher, he actually felt as though there was a human being underneath all the bravado. Philip put a hand on his shoulder and said, 'You did the right thing, Owen.'

He nodded.

'What will happen now?' Philip asked.

'I'm not sure. I know it'll be all over the news before too long, and I'll most likely be arrested, but either way, these children deserve a decent life. I tried my best, but I'm not qualified to help them properly. You were right, Philip. I was awake for most of the night thinking about what you said. They need professional help. I shouldn't have let it go on so long.'

Philip didn't know what would happen to Owen Fisher. He didn't think he would be prosecuted for what he did. As Owen had told him previously, he didn't keep them captive, and he'd even tried to take them home. His only crime was not reporting it, which was still bad, but not bad enough to get him a prison sentence, surely. After all, he fed and clothed them as best he could. He just made a mistake by thinking he could deal with it himself. But he eventually did the right thing. And the children now stood the chance of a decent life.

46

Philip went back into his house. He sat in front of the window, looking up at the lighthouse. His head was still spinning, maybe even more so after seeing how upset Owen Fisher was. He wondered what would happen to him. His aspirations of a political career would be put on hold for a while, that was for sure.

Philip wanted to let things settle in his mind before going to see Charlotte. As he looked up at the lighthouse, he'd realised that he'd already made some important decisions without even thinking about them.

The first decision was to sell his old house. The second was to try and buy the park house. The third was to take Owen Fisher up on his offer of volunteering to run the lighthouse. This would be the perfect place to spend his evenings with his laptop, he thought. And a great way of making sure he'd finally be accepted by the locals.

He also considered investing some money into the town. He wouldn't just hand the money over; he'd want to know what funding Greysands already had first before he offered a philanthropic gift to try to improve the town. He'd given money to many good causes over the years, but he never handed money over without knowing what funding the cause already had available. Investing in Greysands would be no different.

Everything seemed to be working out. He knew where he was, what he was doing and where he was going. He saw no need to stress about the future any more. Things were clear. The only thing he wanted to do was see Charlotte and make his peace with her.

He grabbed his coat and left the house. As he got outside, he put his key in the lock as he always did, but then he stopped. There was no need to lock his doors. Before, he could never walk away from a door without locking it. But today, he felt the urge to leave it unlocked and put his faith in his fellow man. He took his key back out of the lock and walked away.

He went straight to the pub to find that there were quite a few of the locals in there. They all stopped talking as he walked in, much like the first time he'd entered. Only this time, people looked concerned and walked over to him.

'Are you OK, Philip?' Karen said.

'Yes,' he said. 'I'm fine, why?'

'We've seen you on the telly,' the landlord said. 'Terrible what's happened. Are you sure you're OK?'

Philip was flattered by their concern, but he didn't want to talk about it in detail, not at that moment at least.

'I'm fine, honestly.'

He looked around the pub for Charlotte, but he couldn't see her anywhere.

'Is Charlotte here?'

'No. She's off today,' the landlord said.

Philip really wanted to go and see her. It didn't seem appropriate to ask for her phone number, or even her address so he decided to leave it for now.

'OK. I'll catch up with her tomorrow.'

'Let me buy you a drink, Philip,' one of the locals said. A local who he'd spoken to a few times, but not yet learnt his name.

'No. Honestly, I'm fine. Thank you.'

'But you need to know about the amusement park and Councillor Fisher,' Karen said.

'I know all about it,' he said.

This seemed to bring the conversation to an end.

'Are you sure you don't want a drink?' the landlord said.

'No, I'm fine. I appreciate the offer, but I'll catch up with you all later.'

He thanked them again and left the pub.

47

After walking around the town for half an hour or so, hoping to bump into Charlotte, possibly while she was out walking Daisy, Philip decided to concede defeat and head back to his home. Charlotte had told him to sort out his marriage once and for all to give them any chance of starting a relationship, and he'd done that, one way or another. But the way it came to an end might scare her away, he thought. Especially now the news world was telling the story. He badly wanted to see her, but he thought it might be best to leave her be for the time being and let things settle. Maybe once a few days had passed, she'd come around.

He walked along the path leading up to his house. Even though he'd failed to make up with Charlotte, he was still happy to be home. He stopped and turned around to take in the view. The sun was low and the tide was high. He looked all around at the scene in front of him. From the pub on his left, and the arcade at the pier in the distance, all the way around to the beautiful lighthouse building.

Philip was still in a state of shock that he'd caused the death of another human being, but he wasn't going to let that ruin his life. Lesley was ultimately the cause of her own demise. It was her or him, and Philip knew he had nothing to reproach himself for. He'd had no choice but to defend himself.

He rummaged in his pocket for his keys when he suddenly remembered leaving the door unlocked. He smiled to himself as he turned the handle. Once inside, he closed the door, then stopped and stood still as he was greeted by a sound. It was a sound he recognised, but couldn't immediately place. It was like a rattling sound on his wooden floor. He briefly wondered if the creatures had returned. Or maybe they hadn't rounded all the children up during the operation to help them. Or maybe even Twisty and found his way out of the basement.

Then, as all these thoughts quickly shot through his mind, a little grey and white creature came trotting through the living room door and along the hallway.

It was Daisy.

He was as pleased to see her as she was to see him. She spun around him and leaned against his legs as he stroked her. But as pleased to see Daisy as he was, he was even more happy to see Charlotte come through the doorway of the living room and stand there looking at him with an expression he'd never before seen on her beautiful face.

She tilted her head to one side and gave a small smile.

Neither of them spoke as they stood there looking at each other.

Eventually Charlotte said, 'Are you OK?'

Philip laughed a little. 'Never better.'

'I asked you to sort your marriage out, but I didn't realise I was putting you in such terrible danger.'

Philip took a step towards her. 'You didn't put me in danger. I was already in danger. I just didn't know it. But it's done now. It's over.'

She nodded and smiled. A tear slowly ran down her cheek.

Philip didn't think she was sad. It was most likely because of the horrific situation she'd heard about on the news. And maybe also a tear of joy that their relationship could now begin; he wasn't sure.

He couldn't wait any longer. He slowly stepped towards her. She was beautiful. Her hair, her eyes, her smile. He couldn't stop his eyes from dancing all over her face.

As he stood close to her, her gaze lifted to his and her lips parted. He stared into her eyes once more before he finally leaned in to kiss her full on the lips. He knew as he kissed her that this was something he'd been wanting to do ever since he first met her. He was both excited and relieved that not only was she kissing him back, but also, he thought that maybe she'd be a part of his life from now on.

With a powerful, wonderful, strangely heart-warming flood of understanding, he suddenly realised that this mysterious, not-really-at-all-dull seaside town of Greysands was now his home. The park house was now his house. And the lighthouse would be his new venture. The only thing that made those three things ever the more enjoyable, was knowing that he would be sharing it all with Charlotte.

He couldn't believe how much his life had changed. It had only been a few weeks since he was back in Chorley, working hard while oblivious to what his wife and friend were doing and planning. He felt as though he'd won. Not just because he was the only one of them who'd survived, but also because the situation brought him to Greysands and to Charlotte.

After spending the evening together, Charlotte headed home. He promised to woo her as if they were dating for the first time. As much as he wanted to make love to her, he didn't want to disrespect her by taking her straight to bed as soon as they'd reconciled their friendship. He wanted to be respectful and gentlemanly as they embarked on their relationship, so he watched her go home and planned a first date for them; probably a nice restaurant in one of the neighbouring towns. He couldn't wait for her next night off.

48

Considering everything that had happened, and how exhausted he was, Philip didn't expect to still be awake at three in the morning. He'd been going over everything in his mind and he just couldn't switch off. Above everything, there was one thing that Daniel had said that he couldn't get out of his head. It was bouncing around his brain and he just couldn't let it go. He knew he wasn't going to sleep, so he gave in.

He and Daisy walked back down the stairs and went into the living room. After throwing a few logs onto the fire before lighting it, he switched his laptop on. He knew that Daniel was right – he always was about this sort of thing – so Philip had to put faith in him one last time. He laughed to himself that even in death, Daniel was still telling him what to do.

He opened a new file on his computer. He wasn't finished with his Lauren Bates novel, by a long way, but occasionally, when something else entered his mind, he had to break off from his projects to work on something else, and that's what he was doing now.

In the dark living room, lit only by the flickering fire, in the creepy house that was now his home and his inspiration, Philip wrote the heading to a ghostly new story. Perhaps he'd eventually use a pseudonym, but for now, his own name would do.

It read, *The Park House*, by Philip Lloyd.

THE END

ACKNOWLEDGEMENTS

Most stories that find their way into my head start out with a situation. The kernel of an idea that builds and builds, usually as I carry out my everyday routines, or as I try to fall asleep at night.

But Greysands was different. Instead of the story coming to me first, it was actually the town that I couldn't get out of my head.

I've always found the English seaside town a fascinating place to be; especially in winter. They are all made up of the same ingredients. They have a beach, an arcade, shops, and of course a chip shop where you're convinced the fish tastes better as you eat it while looking over the ocean.

In recent years I've become more interested in the people in these towns, wondering if they're actually happy. The few I've spoken to have talked about what boring places they are to live, especially once the summer has ended. Living by the sea is a dream come true for most of us. But it seems that some of the folk lucky enough to have been born there don't actually want to be there. This is one of the many things I find fascinating about these places.

The town of Greysands in my mind is a mixture of several different seaside towns. But for the purpose of this story, the dark side of each one. I always wonder how the businesses survive, especially with the unpredictable weather we have. But somehow, they seem to find a way.

So, as I say, in this book the setting came first before I had any idea of what the story would be. I just started to write to see where it would go and it grew from there.

The finished story isn't that different from the first draft. Apart from some very helpful editing by my very talented agent, James Essinger and some very thorough help from fellow author Marie Campbell.

Which leads me to thank other people who've helped me with this project. Charlotte Mouncey for not only typesetting the book, but also for channelling her inner-self to create a cover that captured the mood of the story perfectly.

And I would also like to thank my wife, Maggi for reading everything I write, and for giving me her honest opinion, no matter how harsh. To quote Lesley Lloyd, *If I don't tell you, your agent will.*

And I would also like to sincerely thank everyone who's supported me so far. Thank you for not only buying my books, but also for being kind enough to take the time to write a review or send me a nice message telling me what you thought. I've had many days where I've not been functioning at my best, when suddenly a message arrives to turn my day around and get me smiling again. For this I will be forever grateful.

And finally, a huge thanks to all at The Conrad Press. It's a great family to be a part of.

BY THE SAME AUTHOR

The Beast of Bodmin

Jo Green is a heroine of the Devon and Cornwall Police.

Thanks to Jo, OCD-plagued chess-player Vladek Boniek is serving thirty years for murdering four women close to Bodmin Moor.

Jo, a police constable at the time, caught him. She's now a detective. Her new career is accompanied by painful realisations about her personal life, which lead to the most serious emotional conflicts she's ever had to face.

Meanwhile, on Bodmin Moor, six months after Boniek's conviction, new killings take place.

Suspicions point to a phantom wild cat.

But is a big cat really the culprit, or is a new Beast of Bodmin on the loose?

ISBN 978-1-911546-36-8